# *Under The*
# *WEEPING*
# *WILLOW*

## MADELEINE PIZZUTI

ISBN: 978-0-6489126-2-0 (paperback)
ISBN: 978-0-6489126-3-7 (e-book)

First published 2022

Cover illustration by Peter Wilks

Book design and typesetting
by Hardshell Publishing
www.hardshellpublishing.com

For enquiries, contact:
Email: maddymissin@yahoo.com
www.madeleinepizzuti.com

Disclaimer: The characters in this book are entirely fictional.
Any resemblance to actual persons living or dead is entirely
coincidental.

Dedicated to the people of Leverington
– the village of my own childhood that holds
so many precious memories.

## CHARACTERS IN *UNDER THE WEEPING WILLOW*

**James McGregor**
Old 'fuddy-duddy' living on the edge of the village who pokes his nose into everything.

**Pamela Yates**
Local librarian in her early thirties - lives next door to James.

**Janet Goodman**
Best friend of Pamela. She works in the school office.

**Marge Saunders**
Village gossip.

**Lorraine Thompson**
Newcomer to the village. Has a daughter who lives in Perth, Australia with her family. Has twin grandsons.

**Sally and James Birchwell**
Retired Publicans.

**Michael Simpson and Karl Basingthwaite**
Publicans of The Shepherd's Arms.

**Jennifer Collins**
Divorcee. Newcomer to the village.

**Tim Collins**
Jennifer's seventeen year old son.

**Father John Morgan**
Parish priest of St Andrew's Church.

**Dr Brendan Jones**
Local General Practitioner.

**Shirley Jones**
Wife of Doctor Brendan.

**Helen Shrewsbury**
Head teacher at the school in her mid fifties. Never married.

**Paul Bloomfield**
Local Pharmacist.

**Sean Blundle**
Local Butcher.

**James Blundle**
Son of Sean the Butcher.

**Rachel and Jack Elam**
Owners of the village shop.

**Betty and Steven Cosgrove**
Farmers, married with two boys – Anthony 14 and Adrian 11.

**Constable Mark Fisher**
Young policeman stationed in the village.

**Natalie and Hans Hoffner**
Dutch-born couple with three children – Mark 14, Juliette 9 and Craig 4.

# CHAPTER 1

M r McGregor bent down slowly to retrieve the battered and rusty rubbish bin lid from the gutter.

"Ooohhh, me back!" he moaned, straightening himself up. "Those lazy council workers haven't got an ounce of common sense. It doesn't take much effort to put the bloody lid back on the bin, does it!" he muttered to himself as he slammed the lid back on his rubbish bin sending a loud, reverberating bang through the early morning peace and quiet of the village.

*Where on earth is everyone*, he thought. It's Saturday morning for heaven's sake. Don't tell me they've all slept in after that dinner dance.

The Lincolnshire village of Toveringham did seem to be unusually quiet for a Saturday morning, especially since it was also market day.

Mr McGregor scanned the street with his squinting eyes for any sign of life before he turned around to carry the bin into his back garden.

"Oh, hello, at least someone's up and about" he spied Pamela, the local librarian, from next door, making her

1

way rather hurriedly to her mini minor parked in her gravelled driveway.

"I can't talk James" she said, stumbling around to the driver's door. "I'm sick … gotta go to the hospital." Just as she said that she doubled over and vomited all over James McGregor's prized petunias!

At the other end of the village, the doctor's surgery was unusually busy for a Saturday morning. The waiting room was full to the brim with some villagers sitting on the garden seat just outside the front. James Blundle, the butcher's lad, was bent right over with his head between his knees. Almost everyone seemed to have the same symptoms – light-headed feeling with nausea and vomiting.

"You okay son?" enquired Dutch-born Hans bending over to see James' face.

"Nooo … not really."

"Mmmm," replied Hans, who did not know what to say to the poor lad, as he brushed past the barrage of patients towards the door of the surgery.

"My word, you sure are pretty busy this morning, lass." Hans commented to the receptionist.

"Good morning, Mr Hoffner. Yes, it is rather. Are you here to pick up your daughter's prescription?"

"Yes, that's right! My wife forgot to collect it when she was here yesterday."

Four doors down at the Shepherd's Arms, Michael and Karl were having a late breakfast. Michael lifted his head from the copy of the Daily Mail that he was reading and stared at his partner of twelve years.

"What's wrong with you this morning? You've spent ages pushing that egg and bacon around on your plate. Come on, out with it."

"I'm fine," Karl responded.

"Oh no you're not. You can't pull the wool over my eyes matey. What's wrong?"

"Oh, I don't know. Maybe it's a virus or something … I just don't feel a hundred percent."

"Are you sick or something? What symptoms have you got?"

"Nothing, just a bit flat, I suppose."

"I know what it is. You're probably in need of a good holiday, we both are. Hey! Let's go up to Mablethorpe for a week. I can get Sally and James to look after the pub, they've done it before … remember?"

Sally and James Birchwell were like mentors to the lads, having kept a public house themselves for fifteen years. They were retired now and would often go travelling, all around the country.

"Oh, don't go bothering them, they're always busy and besides they're probably going away themselves."

"For heaven's sake, they don't go away 24/7, month after month. Surely to goodness we can find a week somewhere where they're free."

Michael stared at his partner waiting expectantly for a reply.

"Well, alright ... ask them. But don't tell them anything about how I feel ... okay?"

"The sea air will do us both good," said Michael, reaching across the table to squeeze his partner's hand.

# CHAPTER 2

As the morning wore on and villagers began to wake up, albeit to moans and groans of upset stomachs, it became evident that the activities of the previous evening had led to an epidemic of food poisoning throughout the village.

Word spread near and far, as quickly as a grass fire; via text messages, phone calls and general gossip.

Lorraine Thompson's phone rang that morning just as she was making her bed.

She dropped the pillow she was plumping up and moved hastily to the phone in her hallway.

"Hello, Lorraine speaking."

"Lorraine, it's Marge. Have you heard what's happened?"

"What … what do you mean … what's happened?"

"You'll never believe it … there's food poisoning right throughout the village."

"Food poisoning! You're kidding!"

"No, I'm not kidding. I've just seen it with my own eyes. I was walking down to Elam's to get the Saturday paper; you know how I always buy it on a Saturday for the crosswords. I think I've told you they have a full page of all sorts of 'em, from real easy to the cryptic ones. Of course, I don't do the real hard ones, but I do have a go at 'em from time to time. Well … (Marge paused for a moment to regain her train of thought) outside the doc's, there they were, practically the whole village queued up to see the doc. I've never seen so many people all looking terribly sick."

"How do you know it's food poisoning?"

"Well, Jenny Elam told me, didn't she? You know how she gets to know everything firsthand, being a shopkeeper and all. It was from that dinner dance they had in the parish hall last night. My word Lorraine, it's lucky we didn't go, you and me, otherwise we'd be sitting right now with the rest of 'em outside the doc's."

"Hmmm," Lorraine wasn't convinced of the accuracy of Marge's news. After all her friend did tend to exaggerate just a little, well actually a lot, if she was truthful.

"Well, that's no good Marge. Let's hope they all get better soon."

Lorraine was happy to end the conversation at that point, but Marge rambled on about the fact that it most definitely must have been the food from the dinner dance. Lorraine held the receiver from her ear, not needing to hear all the details. After about three minutes (which did seem like a lot longer), she decided that she'd heard quite enough gossip for one day, and bringing the receiver back to her ear, announced,

"Well Marge, I'd better go. I've just heard my mobile go off; I'm waiting on a text message from my daughter."

"Oh, that's right! She's coming to visit, isn't she?"

"Yes, see you later Marge!"

And with that Lorraine promptly placed the receiver back into its cradle with a bang.

"Phew!" she breathed a sigh of relief. "That woman can talk. She never lets up."

Lorraine made her way back to the bedroom to finish making her bed, pleased at the fact that she'd been brave enough to cut Marge off before she rambled on too much more.

Smoothing over her duvet, she then turned to kiss the photo of her family that had its permanent place on her bedside locker. She loved them all dearly. After John died, all the family she had left was her only daughter, Suzanne, and her son-in-law, Sam. So, when her twin grandsons arrived it was like a gift from heaven!

Sam was offered a job opportunity in Perth, one which he could not refuse. So, Sam, Suzanne and the twins emigrated to Australia. Lorraine had no other choice than to support them in their decision, after all she wanted them to be happy, and happy they were. The blessing was that at least they could afford to travel back and forth to the United Kingdom every so often due to Sam's highly paid position.

Lorraine hadn't told a white lie to Marge when she said she was waiting on a text message from her daughter, she really was. Suzanne had promised to text her mum when they were about to board the plane at Dubai before the final leg of their journey. Lorraine was so anxious for them, yet at the same time so excited that they were coming home again.

By nine o'clock, market stalls with their brightly coloured striped awnings began to fill the northern end of the village green. There seemed to be fewer stalls than usual, probably due to some stallholders being sick. James Birchwell slammed shut the boot of his station wagon after unloading the last of his home-grown cauliflowers.

"By gum, Jim, they look like good caulies!" remarked Steven Cosgrove, peering over the top of a pile of wooden crates.

"Oh, hello Steve … whatcha up to?"

"Oh, I thought I'd come by early to check out the produce. Here on your own are ya?"

"Yeah, I let the missus sleep in this mornin' after last night's dinner dance. She'll be up later with a flask o' tea and a sandwich."

"Hey Jim, I hear a lot of 'em that went last night are right sick this morning. You should see the line up at the doc's."

"I was wondering why there's so few stalls. Normally by now the green is practically full."

"Well, that'd be why Jim, everyone's sick. By the way, can you put one of those caulies aside for me? I'll pick it up before I go home."

"Sure Steve. See ya later then."

Steve raised his arm to bid farewell whilst Jim stared momentarily at his cauliflowers … wondering whether his wife was okay at home in bed. After all she had gone to the dinner dance on her own last night, leaving Jim to have an early night, seeing as he would have to be up at the 'crack of dawn' this morning.

Dr Brendan Jones had run overtime that morning with his surgery. The majority of cases were in fact food poisoning, some more severe than others.

"In all the years I've been practising here, I've never seen anything like it!" he announced to his receptionist, Mandy. "I'm sure Paul's doing a roaring trade this morning."

Paul Bloomfield was the local pharmacist. He and Brendan had been good mates for many years, arriving at the village almost at the same time, twenty-five years ago.

"Mandy, see that you finish up here soon. You've worked hard this morning."

"Yes, it's been rather hectic, hasn't it? Enjoy the rest of the day Brendan."

"Thanks Mandy, you too."

At that he shut the door of his office and headed out, turning the surgery sign to CLOSED as he left.

# CHAPTER 3

By lunchtime, Pamela, the librarian, had arrived home from the hospital.

"Do you feel any better, lass?" shouted James as she stepped out of her car. Pamela couldn't believe it, the old 'so and so' did seem quite concerned for a change.

Feeling the need to be nice back to him, she cried out, "Sorry about the petunias, James. I'll buy you some fresh ones."

"Oh no need for that, they'll come good, don't worry," he replied.

Pamela raised her hand in acknowledgement and then disappeared through her front door, leaving James standing amongst his garden beds, wondering.

Just then young Adrian Cosgrove rode by on his bicycle.

"Mornin' Mr McGregor," hailed Adrian, "have you heard the news?"

"What news, laddie?"

Adrian squeezed his brake handles and abruptly ground to a halt.

"Food poisoning right throughout the village."

"So, I was right," James murmured to himself.

"You should have seen the queue outside Doc Brendan's surgery, there must have been at least twenty people waiting to see the doc."

James smiled at Adrian and then changed the subject.

"Lord above! That's a mighty fine cauliflower you've got there," nodding at the large item of produce Adrian had in his bicycle basket.

"Yeah, Mr Birchwell put it aside for Dad."

"That'll make a good cauliflower cheese. It'll keep your mum busy this morning, eh lad?"

They both chuckled as James waved young Adrian off home.

A lovely lad, he thought to himself. Pity there's not more like him.

By four o'clock most of the stall holders on the village green were packing up to go home. It had been a long day with fewer than usual villagers out shopping. Most of the customers that day had come from nearby villages. Some of the resident youngsters were now collecting rubbish and doing a general tidy up of The Green. It had been a long-standing tradition for many years to keep the young folk involved in village life. And it seemed to work. Many times, they were rewarded if they'd done a good job with a free orange squash and a hot dog.

Two of the rubbish collectors, Anthony Cosgrove and Mark Hoffner now sat on the wooden garden seat under the willow tree that adorned one end of The Green. Their well-earned hot dogs dripping with tomato sauce were a welcome treat after all that rubbish collecting. They were mates, Anthony and Mark, both in the same year at Ashbury High School.

"I could eat ten of these," said Mark with a mouthful.

"Yeah, they sure do hit the spot," replied Anthony.

"Hey, look over there. Isn't that the new kid that lives in the old thatch? Did you know he goes to our school?"

"How d'ya know that?" enquired Anthony.

"Mum told me. She met his mum at the Women's Institute meeting the other night."

The new kid in the village was now casually kicking around an empty drink can at the other end of The Green.

"I thought we'd cleaned up all the rubbish from that end," said Anthony.

"Maybe it's his own rubbish he's kicking around. Bet he doesn't put it in the bin when he's finished," suggested Mark. "Come on, finish your hot dog and we'll go over there."

The boys finished eating and picked up their already full rubbish bags and wandered over to the other end of The Green. The new boy, who seemed much older closer up, was still kicking around the empty can of drink. He didn't notice the boys approaching and looked up suddenly when they greeted him.

"Hi" said Mark stretching out his hand in welcome. "I'm Mark."

The young man just looked up without saying a word. Noticing the unfriendly response, Anthony didn't bother to introduce himself.

"You're new to the village, aren't you?" asked Mark.

"I guess so," he replied showing little interest in the boys.

"I believe we go to the same school, Ashbury High." Mark continued.

"Is that so?"

"Yep, we're in Year 8. What year are you in?"

"12" came the reply.

Seeing as the conversation wasn't going anywhere and the new young man didn't seem to want to give away much information about himself, Anthony butted in.

"Oh well, we'd better get back to finishing this, maybe we'll see you around some time."

"See ya," he replied and walked off.

"Well, that went well" said Anthony, when the young man was out of earshot.

"Blimey! He didn't even tell us his name."

It was eight o'clock in the evening and Lorraine was washing the dishes in her newly renovated kitchen. Her mobile phone beeped, alerting her that a text message was coming through. She wiped her hands on a tea towel hanging from the oven door, and hurriedly picked up her phone. The message read, "JUST LEAVING DUBAI. ARRIVING EARLY SUNDAY. GET THE KETTLE ON!"

Lorraine smiled with a sense of relief, "God bless them. Keep them safe Lord," she silently prayed.

"Mmmmm ... if they're arriving early tomorrow then I might have to miss church. Well, I'm sure God will understand," she mused.

Lorraine's faith was strong, always had been, even as a child when she imagined she would become a nun. However, when she met John at the age of sixteen, that all changed. *They were destined to be together, forever* she thought. When he was suddenly killed in a road accident on his way home from work, her whole life changed. He was only thirty. They had one daughter, Suzanne. Gone were the dreams of having more children and retiring in Spain, a destination they'd often gone to on holidays.

Lorraine went back to finishing the washing up. Her growing excitement was evident as she began to mentally make plans for the activities she could engage in with her grandsons. This time tomorrow she'd have them all here for dinner, like old times. *I must prepare something nice for them,* she thought, *a lovely roast dinner with Yorkshire pudding. Yes, that's Suzanne's favourite. A roast dinner it is.*

# CHAPTER 4

At nine o'clock sharp the bells of St Andrew's Church, laying nestled in the Bryant Valley, pealed throughout the small village of Toveringham. It was always a welcoming sound to the villagers every Sunday morning, summoning them to worship together. A few latecomers were hurriedly making their way towards the open wooden doors of the church. Some nodded, 'good morning' to Father Morgan as they passed him waiting at the doors, in readiness for the procession down the main aisle of the church. Up in the bell tower, the bell ringers were giving a nod of approval to Hans Hoffner, the new bell ringer, who was learning the ropes (pardon the pun!). It was his first time, ringing the bells of St Andrew's Church, at the commencement of a service, after enduring weeks of tuition every Thursday evening.

"Well done, Hans!" Jack Elam patted Hans on the back. Everyone smiled as they congratulated Hans. It was indeed an honour to be a bell ringer, especially as it seemed to have become a dying art right across the country. However, the villagers of Toveringham were determined to keep it alive.

Meanwhile, Lorraine was in her sitting room re-arranging the cushions on her sofa for the third time, when she heard the sound of the church bells ringing out. She stopped what she was doing and stood still thinking about her obligation to attend Mass on Sundays. It seemed strange to her, missing church. She momentarily felt a pang of guilt. She quickly shrugged the guilt off and went to the window to pull aside the floral curtain, checking to see if there was any sign of her daughter and family. No sign yet. *Still, it might be a while,* she thought to herself, as she mentally calculated how long it would take them to get here from the airport. *If they arrived at six in the morning, surely they'd be here by now? Well, the plane could have been delayed or their luggage could have taken a while to come through.* Lorraine's mind was in a whirl with all these thoughts, combined with nerves and excitement.

Just then she heard a car pull up and she quickly pulled the curtain back again to check who it was. There, outside her front gate was a black London cab looking rather out of place in a small, pretty village such as Toveringham. They were here! She hurried to the door and ran out to greet them.

Lorraine's nerves seemed to dissolve into oblivion as she hugged and kissed them all.

"My word! How you've grown!" she exclaimed, as she held her grandsons close to her.

"It *has* been three years, Mum," clarified Suzanne.

"I know my dear … three long years. Oh, but it's so good to see you all!"

"This is lovely, Mum" said Suzanne as they all made their way to the front door.

"It's real … what do they call it?"

"Chocolate box," added Sam.

"Oh, you know that phrase, do you?" remarked Lorraine, smiling from ear to ear.

"Of course … we watch a lot of ESCAPE TO THE COUNTRY, don't we, Suzanne?"

The three of them laughed.

"Come on in and we'll get you a nice cup of tea and something for the boys, of course," Lorraine bent down again to kiss Jeremy and Joshua on the top of their heads. Sam put their luggage inside the hallway, and they all followed Lorraine into the eat-in kitchen.

"Wow, mum! This is really lovely," Suzanne's eyes scanned the whole kitchen.

"Thank you. I had it done about two months ago. I think I told you."

"Yes, I do remember, but I didn't think it would be this impressive."

"Well, it had to be done as the old kitchen was really pokey and dated, so I decided to extend it."

Lorraine went to put the kettle on, and they spent the next hour or so sitting around the island bench sipping cups of tea and eating fairy cakes whilst watching the boys explore the garden.

# CHAPTER 5

"So, I hear we've got a newly qualified bell ringer in the village" said Michael, the publican at the Shepherd's Arms, to Hans as he slowly pulled the tap handle at the bar.

"There we go, Hans. That's on the house," he placed a schooner of Hans' favourite lager down in front of him.

"That's kind of you Michael."

"Well, I'm all for promoting community involvement and keeping our bells ringing. Look out! Here comes another bell ringer."

Hans turned around to see who was entering the pub.

It was Sally and James Birchwell who lived just outside the village. Sally, it seemed, had not been affected by the food poisoning, although she had attended the dinner dance on Friday without James.

They approached the bar and greeted Hans and Michael.

"Hello Hans. James tells me you did rather well this morning."

"Well, it seemed to go well Sally, and I did get a round of applause from the guys in the belfry."

"I know, I heard them. I was already in the church saving James' seat," replied Sally.

"I didn't know you went to church," butted in Michael, as he casually wiped down the bar.

"Of course, every Sunday. We've got a lot to be thankful for and it doesn't hurt to give up an hour each week to say, 'thanks' to the Almighty."

No comment was made from anyone. Hans took another sip of his lager; Michael continued wiping the bar down, and James changed the subject by placing his order.

In the corner of the bar, near the open fireplace, sat an off-duty police officer, Constable Mark Fisher. He was having a discussion with Helen Shrewsbury, a teacher from the local primary school and Janet Goodman, who worked in the school office.

"I don't know" said Helen, "I really think someone should do something about it. After all, so many people have been affected."

"I agree Helen. Usually after an event like that everyone's in a positive mood and raving on about how good it was. But I've heard nothing but negative stuff from everyone," Janet replied.

"Well, if a formal complaint is to be made about the food poisoning, it needs to go through the relevant legal channels" added Mark. "Ah, here comes Paul."

Helen looked over Mark's shoulder and spotted Paul, the pharmacist, entering the pub. She beckoned him to come and join them.

Paul didn't seem to want to comment much on the food poisoning subject. Instead, the topic of conversation turned to the new family in the village.

However, it wasn't long before a petition was going around the village asking for signatures of anyone who had been affected by the food poisoning.

Patrons had long returned to their homes and Michael and Karl were now tidying up the bar.

"Did you ask them?" enquired Karl.

"Who? Sally and James?"

"Yeah."

"Yes, I did, and they were happy to oblige providing it's not in June as they're visiting their son in Edinburgh. All we have to do is give them a date."

"Mmmm," Karl carried a handful of empty glasses and placed them on the bar.

He was unsure how he felt about them helping out so that he and Michael could have a holiday. After all there was more to it than that.

He'd been carrying this burden on his shoulders for far too long. It was time to tell Michael, and the best place to tell him was away from the distractions of the pub.

# CHAPTER 6

The sun was already up, casting a bright glow into Lorraine's kitchen when she came down the next morning. She carefully closed the double doors to the snug, making sure not to disturb Suzanne and Sam who were sleeping on a pull-out bed. It was early, and Lorraine didn't expect them to be awake just yet, especially since they might be suffering from jet lag.

She went to put the kettle on for a cup of tea but quickly flicked the switch off again as it seemed to be very noisy as it was coming to the boil. *I'll wait until later to do that,* she thought, and instead, very carefully and quietly, set the table for breakfast.

It wasn't long before Suzanne stirred from her sleep and eventually joined her mum in the kitchen. There was so much to catch up on between mother and daughter. After a good fifteen minutes of shared conversation, Suzanne lifted her finger from around the coffee mug, signalling to pause their conversation.

"Do I hear rumblings up above? The boys must be up."

In an instant, Jeremy sheepishly poked his curly head around the half open double doors.

"Come on Jeremy, come and join us darlin," Lorraine patted the kitchen stool inviting him to sit down. "I'll get you some breakfast."

"Where's your brother, Jeremy?" asked Lorraine.

"Toilet" came the reply.

Conversation over breakfast included plans for the day ahead; the touristy places where they could take the boys, and things they'd like to do. They planned to catch a bus into Ashbury in order to hire a car for the duration of their stay. However, not before paying a visit to the village shop owned by Jack and Rachel Elam.

Jack was stacking some shelves with washing powder and detergent when he heard the shop bell ping.

"Good morning, Lorraine! How are you today? Oh! Don't tell me, this must be your family visiting from Australia, am I right?"

Lorraine's face lit up.

"Yes, it certainly is Jack," and Lorraine proceeded to introduce them.

"Well, I do hope you enjoy your stay. You're out for the day, are you?"

"I thought I'd take them out to see Lincoln. The cathedral is lovely and if we're lucky we might see the Punch and Judy Show in the square. The boys, I'm sure, will love that."

"Well, you have a good day out. Is that all for now?" Jack tallied up the few items that Suzanne and Sam had picked out for the road.

"Was that Lorraine's daughter?" enquired Rachel, as she appeared from out the back of the shop, just missing Lorraine and her family.

"She don't half look like her mum, don't you reckon?"

"Yes, I suppose she does a bit," Rachel said as she glared at them through the shop window. "They seem like a lovely family."

Just then the shop bell pinged again, and Pamela Yates came in, seemingly, in rather a hurry.

"Jack, have you got some aspirin? I've got a splitting headache and I'm late opening the library."

"Sure Pamela. Not like you to be late. Are you alright?"

"I'm still not one hundred percent after that dreadful food poisoning."

"Oh, by the way Pamela," butted in Rachel. "Talking about food poisoning, there's a petition pinned on the noticeboard outside. It seems the Parish Council have taken it upon themselves to make a formal complaint about the whole incident. It asks for those who were affected to sign the petition. Feel free to sign it on your way out if you like."

"I might just do that," Pamela agreed, and off she went in a flurry.

She always seems to be in a hurry these days, Jack thought to himself, as he watched Pamela disappear out the door, and yet the funny thing was, she was always composed and methodical when she went about her business in the library.

His thoughts then returned to the stacking of the shelves.

"By the way, Rachel, have you seen or heard much about that new family in the village? You know, the one in old Charlie's thatched cottage."

"Well, I did see her at the Women's Institute meeting the other week. What's her name? Marjorie … no … Jessica … no … I'll get it in a minute."

Rachel went mentally through the alphabet trying to remember the woman's name, whilst Jack rambled on about something or other.

Then suddenly she shouted out "JENNIFER! That's it!"

"Good grief woman! Why do you do that every time?"

"It's the only way I can figure out someone's name, by going through the alphabet." She smiled at her husband, content that she had used her analytical skills to solve yet another memory lapse regarding names.

# CHAPTER 7

The mild spring weather was a welcome relief after the harsh winter that Toveringham had experienced. The days were now sunny, with a gentle breeze from time to time, allowing the brilliant yellow daffodils to nod their heads at passers-by.

The feathery leaves of the weeping willow swayed gently in the breeze as if they had not a care in the world. The willow tree on The Green was a favourite spot to sit under… its green canopy giving shade and shelter. A wooden bench had been placed there some years ago enabling villagers and tourists alike to sit awhile. There was also a small duck pond near the willow tree attracting birds and wildlife throughout the year.

Thankfully the weather had been kind to Suzanne, Sam, and the twins, enabling them to go out most days and really enjoy their holiday. The twins and Sam had spent a great time kicking a ball around on The Green and going for a ramble on the edge of the village meandering along the country lanes. It gave Suzanne and her mum quality time to spend together, learning about life in Perth and about Lorraine's involvement in village life, the friends she had made (even the gossipy ones like Marge!). Lorraine loved having her family around. It gave her the opportunity to spoil her grandsons ... as was a grandma's prerogative.

However, at the back of her mind was the lurking reality that she would eventually have to say 'goodbye' to them when their holiday came to an end.

The six weeks she would have with them, would no doubt fly by.

As the time grew closer to their departure date Lorraine would lie in bed at night fighting back tears at the mere thought of them leaving. It seemed her whole life was made up of 'goodbyes'. The time that she lost her husband prematurely; when she sold her family home and moved to the country leaving friends behind; and when Suzanne and her family emigrated to Perth.

It was the last weekend before Suzanne and her family were due to leave, so Sam and Suzanne were enjoying a stroll through the market on the village green. Lorraine was back at the cottage preparing their lunch and minding the boys.

"You know your mum is going to find it difficult on Monday when we have to leave," said Sam.

"I know ... so am I" Suzanne replied.

Sam put his arm around her waist and kissed her on the cheek.

"Hey! Let's get your mum some flowers. There's a flower stall over there." Sam grabbed Suzanne's hand and pulled her over in the direction of the stall. Suzanne loved the thoughtfulness of her husband; it was one of his finer attributes.

"We've brought you some flowers, Mum," Suzanne announced as they walked straight into the kitchen on their return from the market. Lorraine looked up from what she was doing, saw the two of them standing there holding a large multi-coloured bunch of foxgloves, peonies and cornflowers when her tears began to fall.

"Oh Mum!" Suzanne went to comfort her mum leaving Sam to hold the flowers. The twins ran in from the garden at that very moment and both came to an abrupt standstill on seeing their mum and grandma in tears.

"Why are you all crying?" questioned Joshua, with a shocked look on his face.

Sam quickly reassured the boys that all was okay and that sometimes mums and grandmas need to cry from time to time.

"Oh" they both replied and returned to their soccer game outside.

# CHAPTER 8

"Hi Pamela. Are you ready to go to lunch?"

"Hi Janet. Yeah, give me a minute to shut down here and I'll meet you under The Willow."

"Okay. I'll grab a sandwich from Elam's whilst you're doing that, and I'll meet you over there."

Janet and Pamela were great friends. They were both single and in their mid-thirties with no desire to get married, settle down and have children. Janet worked in the school office across the road and the two of them often met for lunch … either on The Green or in the Shepherd's Arms.

Janet walked briskly over to Elam's, bought a ham, cheese and tomato sandwich on brown bread, and then joined Pamela on the seat under The Willow.

"I see they've got a petition up at the shop for the food poisoning thing."

"Yeah, Rachel asked me if I'd sign it."

"And did you?"

"You bet I did. It's taken me a week or so to get over it and I still don't feel a hundred percent. I woke up this morning with a splitting headache."

"How's it now?"

"I took some aspirin."

"Are you busy in the library?"

"So, so. Had the weekly visit from Sefton Primary this morning, the infants this time."

"What about you?"

"Well, good for a Monday morning I suppose. You know how Carol Cruikshank retired last term. Well, we still haven't filled her position. However, today someone came for an interview, she's had years of experience in teaching high school but now wants to go primary. Guess who it was?"

"Who?"

"Jennifer Collins, the new woman in the thatched cottage."

"Really?"

"Yeah. Anyway, she seemed quite nice and talkative too. I don't know whether she'll get the job or not, there's still a couple more interviews to go before they decide."

Pamela decided to change the subject.

"How's the sandwich?"

"Not bad."

They both stayed comfortably chatting under The Willow almost forgetting they had to return to work when Janet suddenly caught a glimpse of Pamela's watch.

"Good grief … is that the time? I must get back … it's almost two o'clock. See you tonight at the Arms for a drink?"

"Yeah, no problem … usual time?"

"Yeah. See ya Pam."

And Janet grabbed her bag from the seat and sped off back to the school office, leaving Pamela to get rid of the discarded sandwich bag she'd left behind.

That evening at the Shepherd's Arms, Janet and Pamela were amongst just a few patrons. It was unusually quiet for a Monday evening. They sat in their favourite spot close to the open fire, which Michael had lit, seeing as it was rather a cool evening.

"Has your headache gone?" enquired Janet.

"Yes, thank goodness," Pamela took a sip of her lemon squash.

"You know, when I went home this afternoon that silly old fool was in his front garden again. It's almost like he knows when I'm coming home and just waits for me. It's really annoying!"

"Oh, the poor man's probably lonely, he doesn't seem to get out much, does he? You never really see him in the village or in the shop, do you?"

"No. He keeps to himself and just bothers me!"

"You know, you should ask him over for a cuppa, you might find him okay … poor Mr McGregor."

"Yeah sure," Pamela's tone of voice was not that of someone who was convinced it was a good idea.

The fact was it was true. James McGregor was lonely. He spent most of his week at home just tending occasionally to his garden and looking out for Pamela's return from work. Once a week he would catch the bus that would take the elderly into Ashbury to do their weekly shop, and that was all. He never went anywhere else. Many people didn't have time for James, most of the villagers had labelled him as 'old and grumpy'. The truth was that he *was* old and grumpy. But people don't just get old and grumpy overnight. James' loneliness was the cause of him being grumpy.

He had lived in Scotland for most of his life. As a youngster he was a real hit with the girls, being handsome with dark, wavy hair and quite tall. What was left of his hair now resembled the colour of snow and he was bent over with arthritis. Back in his early twenties he married his childhood sweetheart, and after some years of trying for a family, they finally had a daughter, Cheryl. She was their pride and joy and the 'apple of James' eye'. Sadly, Cheryl died from cancer at the age of twenty-five. James' world was shattered. Shortly after Cheryl's death he and his wife moved to Toveringham for a fresh start. He then fell into deep depression, and when he lost his wife a few years later, it was the end of the world for James. Sadly, he was never able to recover from the grief of losing his wife and his daughter and opted to live the life of a virtual recluse.

James had no living relatives left in the United Kingdom, and so looked upon Pamela, next door, as the daughter he should still have. Looking out for her every afternoon and trying to converse with her whenever the opportunity arose. This was his way of keeping the memory of his own daughter alive. Pamela, however, was unaware of all of this.

# CHAPTER 9

With the milder weather setting in, it wasn't long before morning frost gave way to budding spring flowers; crocuses, snowdrops, daffodils, and bluebells began to decorate the front gardens of almost every cottage in the village.

Lorraine Thompson's family had long returned to Australia; Michael and Karl had yet to set a date for their holiday, and the official investigation into the village food poisoning fiasco was ongoing. It had been determined, via outside investigators, that the contaminated food was in fact a particular type of ham. The ham was a part of the entrée, of which some attendees had eaten at the dinner dance.

The sun was just starting to peep over the horizon when Jack Elam unlocked the front door of his shop. The village was covered in darkness except for the glow of a few streetlights. He yawned heavily and stood in the doorway with his arms folded to ward off the early morning chill. Any minute now his delivery of milk, yogurt and perishables would arrive. "There he is," Jack murmured to himself.

He could see the light of the emerging delivery van's headlights coming around the corner.

"Mornin' Jack. How's it going?" the delivery driver jumped down from his cab and headed towards the back of his van. He pulled open the large back doors exposing the neatly assembled cartons and bottles of milk.

"A bit chilly this morning" replied Jack. "Here's hoping it turns out to be a fine day."

The two of them unloaded Jack's order into the shop and the delivery driver then went on his way. "See you on Friday, Jack."

"Okay, will do."

Within half an hour of Jack's early start, the village turned from cold, dark streets to bright spring sunshine warming every corner, along with the sounds of nature in perfect harmony. Cows could be heard in the distance; a cock was crowing, and birds were in full swing with their morning song.

For years Toveringham had been designated a picturesque village that seemed to appeal to visitors and tourists. One could easily understand why. It was a village that made motorists slow down and take in its beauty whilst passing through it. The village was nestled in the Bryant Valley surrounded by green patchwork fields, dotted with long-fleeced sheep and Lincoln Red cattle.

The entrance to the village was over a stone bridge that lay across the River Wenn. Once over the bridge, there would be so many fascinating sights for the eye to see. There were the thatch-roofed alms-houses; the village green with its majestic willow tree; the thirteenth century St Andrew's church and its impressive belltower; the Shepherd's Arms with its outdoor garden area and the village corner shop with its large bay windows filled with colourful merchandise. Oh, and not forgetting the pretty front gardens that lined the main street, one of which was James McGregor's, of course!

It wasn't long before word got out that there was a new teacher at the school. Yes, Jennifer Collins got the job, and apparently seemed to be fitting in rather well. In fact, she had fitted very well into village life. She, and her son, Tim, had moved to the village just a month prior from the outskirts of London. Her divorce from her husband had been rather traumatic and she wanted a fresh start. Her other two sons were married, but Tim, being the youngest was still living at home. It had been a difficult move for Tim as he had left his friends behind, and it was also his last year at high school. However, Jennifer made the rather rash decision to move, seemingly thinking more of her own needs than anyone else's. Tim's brothers didn't have much to do with

Jennifer, the divorce seemed to split the family in two, and they now favoured their father's side of the family. Jennifer hadn't heard from either of her boys for almost two years.

It was the end of Jennifer's first week in her new position teaching third form.

The luxury of being able to walk to and from work was a real joy compared to the traffic jams she had to cope with in London. It only took her five minutes to walk home and that was at a slow pace. She pushed her front gate open and stopped to smell the roses growing around her front door. She knew they didn't have a scent, but it was sheer habit to bend down and smell them. Tim wouldn't be home from school just yet, the bus he caught from Ashbury usually passed through the village at 4.15 pm. She dropped her bags in the hallway and went to the kitchen to make a cuppa and put her feet up for a bit. Standing in front of a class for most of the day was something she hadn't done in a while. It would take a bit of getting used to again. Jennifer was just beginning to nod off with a mug of tea in her hands when she heard Tim's key turn in the door. She prised herself from the comfort of her chair and placed her empty mug on the coffee table.

"Tim, is that you?"

There was no answer.

As Jennifer slowly moved towards the hallway, she saw Tim standing near the bottom of the staircase with his hand on the balustrade ready to go upstairs. He looked his mother straight in the face and with aggression in his voice said, "I hate that school. In fact, I hate this whole place!" and promptly marched upstairs to his room.

Jennifer's feeling of contentment, having spent a good first week in her new job, was now ruined by Tim's outburst, as worry and anxiety now began to set in.

Dinner was a rather quiet affair. Jennifer didn't want to start an argument or anything, she had had quite enough of that with her ex-husband. She was tired of arguments, it was now time for peace and serenity, but something told her it was not going to be that easy.

The following Sunday Jennifer attended the church service at St Andrew's. She was keen on getting to know the people in the village and going to church was one way of doing that. She had already been to a Women's Institute meeting which she thoroughly enjoyed and met many of the local women of the village, some of whose names she'd already forgotten. As she sat in her pew in the church, she casually looked around at the variety of parishioners who were there. She noticed one girl from her own third-form class who was attending with her parents. She made a mental note to go and say hello after the service. Jennifer was well known for acting on the spur of the moment and after she'd made a point of getting to know the third-form family at the conclusion of Mass, she made a beeline for Father Morgan who was outside chatting to parishioners. She hovered around him waiting for the last person to shake his hand and then she put her own hand out to say hello.

"Hello Father Morgan. Do you remember me? Jennifer Collins from Twickenham parish."

"Oh, my word, so it is! How are you? What are you doing here in Toveringham?"

"Well, my husband and I broke up and I moved here to start afresh."

"Oh, I'm so sorry to hear about you and your husband. What about the boys?"

"Tim is with me. The others are married now."

"Are you working?"

"Yes, I'm teaching right here at the primary school."

"Oh, I did hear that there was a new teacher at the school, I didn't imagine it would be you though."

Jennifer smiled. "Father, could I possibly have a word with you about something?"

"Certainly, now or privately?"

"Well privately if that's possible."

"Sure. Why don't you ring during the week and make an appointment? The presbytery number is in the parish bulletin." He pointed to the bulletin which Jennifer had in her hand.

"Will do, thank you so much," and they shook hands again.

# CHAPTER 10

The very next morning in her morning tea break, Jennifer made the call to the presbytery to make an appointment for that afternoon, after school finished.

She managed to dismiss her students fairly quickly, and without getting caught up in 'chatty' conversations with the parents, she moved swiftly to her appointment with Father Morgan. As she made her way towards the presbytery, which was on the other side of the school building, she wondered whether people would notice her and start asking questions. She quickly brushed that thought aside and continued towards Father Morgan's door. A brass bell hung from the beams covering the front porch. She struck it a few times to alert Father Morgan of her arrival.

"Hello Jennifer. Do come in"

She was greeted by a very casual-looking Father Morgan dressed in baggy jeans and a polo shirt.

"Please excuse my attire won't you. It's my day off."

Jennifer smiled.

Father Morgan ushered her into the front office.

"Please take a seat."

Jennifer approached a very antique looking green, leather-padded armchair which seemed as though it had seen better days. She tentatively sat down feeling as if she was going to slide off it onto the floor at any minute.

"How are you settling in at the school?" Father Morgan enquired.

"Very well thanks. The staff are really helpful and the children, of course are just a joy, though I've quickly sorted out who are the naughty ones." They both laughed.

"I can just imagine."

After a short pause, he continued. "Now how can I help you today?"

Jennifer proceeded to explain how she had come to live in Toveringham with Tim for a fresh start after her divorce. She then went on to ask if he knew of any way that Tim could become more involved in village life to help him adapt to their new way of living.

She concluded by saying, "I'm worried that if I don't do something to help him now, that he will get very depressed."

"I see." Father Morgan gave a deep sigh, and at that moment she hoped she hadn't become a burden by asking such a question of him.

"Have you considered him getting maybe a small, part-time job in the village or somewhere nearby? Possibly helping in a shop or even the pub. Perhaps the

Shepherd's Arms might be interested in hiring someone to wipe down the tables or do other odd jobs."

"Well, I hadn't thought of that. Yes, maybe that's an idea. It's worth a try, I guess."

However, Jennifer wasn't too convinced that working in a pub would be a good idea for her son.

Jennifer and Father Morgan continued discussing the matter, bouncing back and forth a few ideas, until it was time to go.

"Thank you, Father Morgan. I really appreciate your help with this. Jennifer moved towards the door.

"You're welcome, Jennifer, anytime. Let me know how you go, won't you?"

"Yes, I will."

# CHAPTER 11

Over the next few weeks Jennifer mulled over the suggestions from Father Morgan and wondered how she might approach Tim with the idea of getting a job.

One Sunday, Tim had left the house after breakfast and went wandering around the village, instead of hibernating in his room. Meanwhile Jennifer stood at the kitchen sink washing the breakfast dishes. She had a lovely view of the village green right across the road from her cottage, and through the kitchen window she spotted Tim sitting under the weeping willow. It was at that moment that she suddenly thought it was the best time to approach Tim about possibly getting a casual job in the village. She quickly pulled off her apron, grabbed the front door key and wandered nonchalantly over to where Tim was sitting under the willow. He looked up briefly as his mother approached.

"It's peaceful under here, isn't it?" she was hopeful in starting up a conversation with her son.

Tim just muttered, "mmm" with his head down, looking at the grass beneath his feet. They sat there for some time without any words being exchanged. Then Jennifer took the plunge.

"Tim, I've been thinking. I know it's been hard for us moving here and you moving away from your friends and all that. You know that I said it would only be until you finished school and got a job, then you could move to wherever you wanted. You don't have to live at home forever." There was silence. "In the meantime, why don't you get a small part-time job, perhaps in the village, it might do you the world of good. You could make friends and earn a bit of money at the same time."

"You've got to be kidding! There's no way I'm getting a job in this dump of a place."

Jennifer froze. She couldn't reply to Tim's reaction to her suggestion. Anymore words from her might ignite an argument and that's one thing she didn't want, especially not there on the village green!

Jennifer was right. Someone did notice her visiting Father Morgan on that Monday afternoon after school. It happened to be Marge Saunders, of all people, and of course she couldn't resist telling everyone about it!

"Mornin' Rachel!" Marge burst into the shop on Tuesday morning.

"Mornin' Marge. How's things?"

"Oh, pretty good, thank you Rachel. I'm after some flowers for Lorraine, it's her birthday and I'm taking her out to lunch."

"Oh, that's lovely. Where are you off to?"

"The Blackfriars Inn at Ashbury."

"Jack and I have been there a few times; they've changed hands recently and I believe the food is really delicious now. What are you after, Marge … some roses, or maybe a mixed bunch?"

"I think the yellow roses would be ideal, don't you?"

Rachel took the roses out from the aluminium bucket and shook the excess water off the stems, then wrapped them carefully in clear cellophane wrap. She finished it off with a pastel green bow tied around the stems.

"That'll be five pounds thanks Marge."

As Marge handed over a five pound note she leant across the counter and in a half whisper said, "Do you know much about that new family in the thatched cottage?"

"You mean the new teacher at the school?"

"Yes, that's the one."

"No, not really, apart from her coming into the shop to buy her lunch from time to time."

"Well … I saw her the other day going into Father Morgan's, straight after school it was. The children had hardly left their classrooms when I saw her head towards his door. She must have been there a while because I got caught up talking to Betty Cosgrove outside the butchers, and by the time I'd finished with Betty there had been no sign of her leaving Father Morgan's. I had a bird's eye view, you see, from where I stood talking to Betty." Marge gave a rather significant '*there you go*' type of nod of her head as she completed her story.

"Well, who knows why she went to see Father Morgan. Anyway, it's none of our business Marge. Now, is there anything else I can get you?"

Rachel quickly changed the subject making Marge feel frustrated as always. However, Rachel was right, it was none of their business and Rachel was not one for getting herself caught up in a lot of gossip.

# CHAPTER 12

Rain clouds began to gather over the valley. It was the beginning of summer and it seemed as if a storm was brewing. A blustery wind was beginning to blow making the willow tree's boughs sway in the wind. It was also playing havoc with Helen Shrewsbury's dress as a gust of wind suddenly caught it, leaving nothing to the imagination! She hoped Paul, the pharmacist, hadn't noticed her struggle with her dress blowing up as she approached the pharmacy door. She breathed a sigh of relief as she entered the shop quickly smoothing down her windswept hair.

"A bit windy out there, isn't it Helen?" Paul remarked from behind the counter.

"It sure is. There must be a storm coming."

Helen was the head teacher at the school. She had never married and was a rather young looking fifty-five.

Paul smiled as she tidied her hair and made sure her dress was all in order.

"I'm after some hair colour Paul. I usually buy L'Oreal, but it seems they don't make my colour anymore. I think I'll have to get another brand."

Helen followed Paul to where the hair treatment stand was located, in the far corner of the shop.

"This brand is probably the closest to L'Oreal in quality and price. I'll let you have a browse at the colours."

Paul Bloomfield was tall with almost totally grey hair. He was in his late fifties and had never married (though one would wonder why as he seemed such a charming and pleasant fellow). He'd arrived in the village at almost the same time as Dr Brendan Jones, the local general practitioner. They'd quickly become friends through their shared interest in the general health of the village and would sometimes go fishing together when they managed a weekend off.

"There we are. This looks like a close enough colour." Helen placed the box of hair colour onto the counter.

"I expect you're glad the food poisoning fiasco is over now, Paul. You must have been rather busy here over that weekend, filling prescriptions?"

"Yes, it was rather busy. Were you affected by it?"

"No. Would you believe at the last minute I decided not to go. A good friend, whom I hadn't seen in a while, turned up on my doorstop that afternoon and I didn't have the heart to tell her to leave."

"Well in hindsight it was probably a good thing she did come over," Paul gave Helen one of his warm, charming smiles.

# CHAPTER 13

"Now don't forget the delivery is on Mondays now, around nine o'clock. Any problems don't hesitate to ring the brewery, you've got the number." Michael's instructions to Sally and James regarding the operation of the pub had been endless and they were eager to see the boys off so that they could get on with things.

"Okay, now you two go and enjoy yourselves and relax for a couple of weeks. We'll be okay here."

"Now you've got our mobile numbers in case of an emergency, haven't you?"

"Yes, but there won't be any, so don't go worrying."

"Thanks so much for this," interrupted Karl. "We really appreciate it."

"You're welcome, now go!"

Karl and Michael had packed up the Range Rover earlier with their suitcase, and now they tooted the horn to Sally and James as they drove out of their driveway and headed to Mablethorpe.

"Well, here we are, my love. Back behind the bar again." James put his arm around his wife and gave her a kiss on the cheek.

"It reminds me of old times. What do you reckon, James?

"Yep, sure does. Come on we'd better get a move on. It'll be opening time before we know it."

Mablethorpe was just what Michael and Karl needed. It wasn't too crowded for the time of the year; the weather was perfect for August and really good for long walks on the promenade. Karl realised that this was probably the easiest place to speak to Michael, away from the pub. He was tired of carrying this burden on his shoulders and he couldn't hide it from his partner much longer. It was eating at him from the inside and it showed on the outside. Michael had sensed there was something Karl was keeping to himself, and he didn't like it. After all they'd known each other for twelve years and there were no secrets between them. They booked into a hotel across from the seafront, which had been recommended to them by Sally and James. After a good night's sleep and a hearty full-English breakfast the next morning, the pair headed off to the Seafront Markets to check out the local delicacies.

# CHAPTER 14

Back in Toveringham, Pamela and Janet had arranged to meet under the Willow for lunch.

"Here, try some of this Janet. I made it last night, it's a pasta bake. It's still warm, I just heated it up in the microwave." Janet took the small container and plastic fork that her friend had packed for her.

"Yum, it looks good."

"I took some over to James before I left for work this morning."

"You did what?" in shock, Janet turned to face Pamela.

"I thought you didn't like the old guy."

"Well, I've been thinking a bit about what you said and how I should invite him over for a cuppa, and, well it got the better of me and I thought the pasta bake might cheer him up a bit. I guess it was a moment of weakness."

"I wouldn't say that Pam."

The two paused for a moment thinking about Pamela's actions."

"Actually, I'm very proud of you."

"You are?" Pamela looked surprised.

"Yes, I am. And what did he say?" eager to know the result of her friend's kindness.

"Well, he looked a bit shocked and then took the dish from me and a big smile came across his face, showing all his rotten teeth that I'd never seen before, as he never smiles!"

The two of them burst into a fit of laughter, struggling to keep their lunches on their knees.

"Watch out!" Pamela cried out. "You'll soon be feeding the birds with your pasta bake!"

After they'd calmed down from all the laughing, Janet asked, "Well, are you still going to invite him over for a cuppa?"

"I might do. I'll see if he likes my pasta bake first and then in a couple of weeks, I'll have him over."

"You know this pasta bake's pretty good Pam; you should make it more often."

# CHAPTER 15

"A pint of bitter please, Sally."

Constable Mark Fisher grabbed a vacant bar stool and made himself comfortable at the bar. He was off duty now and ready for some winding down after a busy day of endless paperwork.

Sally pulled a pint and placed it on the bar.

"Thanks Sally. How's it all going then?"

"Oh, not too bad Mark. You know, once you've done it before it seems to all come back to you after a while."

Sally and James had run the Black Goose in Ashbury for ten years when their children were young. It had been hard work, what with two boys to attend to, as well as running a pub. However, they did it and they loved it. It had been a dream of James' to run a pub, more *his* dream than Sally's.

It had been several months since the evening of the village dinner dance, when it was confirmed that forty people who attended (including two band members from outside the village) had contracted food poisoning. Although the forty had well and truly recovered from the unfortunate incident, the whole event had been marred. The number of signatures on the petition at Elam's shop was a good indication of how people felt about the whole thing.

A solicitor had been appointed to act on behalf of the Parish Council, and Sean Blundle, the local butcher and President of the Council (whose own son had been affected by the food poisoning), was acting as a representative in court.

It didn't take long for the word to get around that Jennifer Collins had paid a visit to Father Morgan, due to the gossiping prowess of Marge Saunders.

Meanwhile Jennifer's concern over her son's inability to adapt to the village was growing. Tim had become more withdrawn, shutting himself away in his bedroom most evenings and only speaking to his mum whenever it was absolutely necessary. Jennifer felt she was walking on eggshells. She feared opening her mouth to start a conversation in case it led to an argument. At times it felt like she was living on her own.

School was finished for the day and Jennifer had decided to stay back and catch up with some marking when her mobile phone rang. She rummaged in her bag trying to find her phone, thinking it might be Tim calling her.

The screen displayed PRIVATE NUMBER.

"Hello, Jennifer speaking," she answered cautiously.

It was Tim's Principal. He had called to say how he was a little concerned over Tim's behaviour in school, and, being aware of the family history, wondered whether he should have some counselling. Jennifer already knew the suggestion of counselling would go down like a 'lead balloon'. There was no way she was even going to suggest it. She was beginning to think their move to Toveringham was a bad choice. *Had she been selfish in her decision to move, especially to the country? Was she only thinking of her own needs and not Tim's? Was this yet another example of her inability to see past herself and her own selfish desires?*

Jennifer slipped her phone back into her bag at the end of the call and dropped her head into her hands. Tears soon began to fall, and she scanned the room for the box of tissues that always seemed to disappear off her desk during the day.

Suddenly the classroom door burst open. It was Janet.

"Oh, I'm sorry for bursting in, Jennifer! I didn't know you were still here. I just wanted to borrow that list of students I gave you this morning. I need to enter their names in the … are you alright?" she asked.

"Yes, I'm fine."

"Are you sure?"

"Yes, just got a bit of a cold," she quickly shrugged off the question.

"Is it okay … to borrow the list?"

"Yes sure, it's here somewhere."

Jennifer retrieved the list from under some papers on her desk and handed it to Janet, who made a quick exit, thanking Jennifer on the way out. She was almost sure something was troubling Jennifer.

# CHAPTER 16

The first week of Karl and Michael's holiday break had been really enjoyable. They had visited art galleries, markets of every description and enjoyed evening meals at various restaurants in the area. Karl hadn't wanted to spoil the whole holiday, so he didn't say anything to Michael during their first week of holidays. However, he knew that the longer he left it the harder it would be to say anything.

The pair had just eaten at an Italian restaurant and were now enjoying a stroll along the Mablethorpe promenade. It was a pleasant evening with a slight breeze coming off the sea. The mood between them was peaceful and harmonious and Karl found it hard to speak, knowing that his words would most certainly spoil this perfect evening. Yet he must say something.

Pausing to watch the sun slowly disappear over the horizon, they both leant on the railings of the pier to watch the seagulls swooping down below near the surface of the water. Without looking up Karl spoke.

"I need to talk to you, Michael."

"I was wondering when you were going to."

Karl stood silently, wondering how to proceed.

"You know how I've been doing my family tree … for a while now."

"Mmmm."

"Well, I've discovered something which is rather upsetting."

"What? Is one of your ancestors a convict? Guilty of murdering someone?" he gave a smirk as he looked at Karl.

"It's much more than that."

On hearing that statement Michael turned to look at Karl. The lines on his face suddenly made him look weathered and older.

Karl continued, "You remember that day, a couple of months ago, when I went to Cambridge to look up some stuff?"

"Yeah"

"I checked up at the Births, Deaths and Marriages place. I wanted to see the entry for my mum and dad. Well, it confirmed that they had two children, me and my sister Cathy of course, but I also found out that Mum had another baby before me when she was sixteen, it was a boy."

"You're kidding!"

"She wasn't married of course so she put the baby up for adoption."

"But didn't your mum tell you any of this when she was alive?" Michael butted in.

"No. I've only ever known about me and Cathy."

"Go on," Michael was keen to hear more.

"Well, the adopted child was born in Worthing … and his name is Michael Bartholomew."

"WHAT!"

Michael's face went red in horror. It couldn't be … could it? *His* name was Michael Bartholomew Simpson. He always knew he was adopted; his parents had talked to him about it when he was young. He had taken on the surname of his adoptive parents, Simpson, but they had continued to call him Michael Bartholomew which was the name given to him at birth. How many Michael Bartholomews could there be, for heaven's sake! Bartholomew certainly wasn't a common name.

Michael looked stunned. He stared out at the horizon, where the sun was almost about to disappear. Its glow sent a bright yellow flicker across the surface of the water. The sun seemed to be disappearing in his life at this very moment.

"I'm worried, Michael. It can't be, can it?"

"Heck! I certainly don't want it to be!"

"If this is true, it means that you and I …"

"Good grief I know! You don't have to spell it out." Michael yelled back at Karl.

"I've got to sit down." Michael headed for the nearest bench. Karl followed behind. The pair sat in silence for what seemed like an eternity. Then Michael spoke.

"I have to see this with my own eyes, Karl."

"That's okay. I can come with you if you like."

Michael didn't answer. This was news that shocked the both of them. No wonder Karl had not seemed himself lately, carrying this burden on his shoulders, wondering when to break the news to Michael.

The next morning, they decided to cut their holiday short and go to Cambridge so that Michael could see the documents which would confirm the devastating news. If it was true, then Michael and Karl were in fact half-brothers.

# CHAPTER 17

"Ooohh lassie, it was very tasty!" said Mr McGregor as he handed the empty dish back to Pamela. It was Saturday morning and Pamela was in the middle of baking some muffins when she heard the doorbell ring. She'd just managed to put the muffin tray into the oven, drop the oven mitts onto the kitchen bench and then hurry to answer the door. There he was, this small figure of a man bent over with age and precariously holding the pasta bake baking dish in his hands.

"Oh, hello James. I'm glad you liked it." Pamela took the dish from his hands and motioned for him to come in.

"Would you like to come in for a cuppa? I've just put some muffins in the oven to bake."

James hesitated with his answer, then replied. "Well, that would be lovely, thank you."

He followed Pamela into the kitchen, and she pulled out a chair for him at the kitchen table.

"Excuse the look of the kitchen, James. I'm a bit messy when it comes to cooking."

"Oh, that's alright! At least you can cook." He smiled at her showing those rotten teeth again. She had a funny feeling that she'd be seeing a lot more of those teeth from now on, now that they'd started to become friendly neighbours.

"How do you go for cooking for yourself James?" Pamela enquired, as she filled the kettle up to boil.

"Oh well, I get Meals on Wheels during the week and then I try to fend for myself on the weekend. I must admit, I miss having Cheryl around."

"Cheryl?" Pamela placed a bone China cup and saucer on the table in front of James.

"She was my daughter. She looked after me really well when her mum was sick and unable to cook for us. She was a great cook, was Cheryl."

The kettle whistled loudly, interrupting their conversation. Pamela seemed deep in thought as she poured boiling water into the teapot. She sat down at the table to join James.

"Forgive me for prying James, but did you say Cheryl is no longer with you?"

"She passed away from cancer."

"Oh, I'm so sorry." Pamela quickly responded. "Was she your only child?"

"Yes, we didn't have any more, it took us a while to have her."

For the first time in many years James McGregor found himself sharing the story of his life and his heartache with someone, and that someone happened to be Pamela. She was remarkably attentive to what James had to say. In fact, she found his story interesting, and at the same time, rather sad. As she learnt more about James and his history, she began to see another side to this "grumpy old man" with rotting teeth. A gentler personality began to emerge at the kitchen table that Saturday morning, which was not at all how he portrayed himself to others.

As Pamela watched James make his way back across her gravelled driveway to his home next door, after enjoying a pleasant cuppa and chat, she thought about how she would describe the whole encounter to her best friend, Janet.

# CHAPTER 18

The village was all abuzz with the upcoming Annual Cricket Match – Ladies versus Men. Bets were being taken in the Shepherd's Arms as to who would win the trophy this year, and Elam's shop had a registration form for anyone who was interested in joining the teams. Training for both teams had begun, and this year there seemed to be more interest than usual. This was possibly because the young people of the village were growing up into their teens and seemed to have a more competitive streak now that they were that much older. Steven Cosgrove, a farmer from just outside the village was the chief co-ordinator of the event and he also had his two sons, Adrian and Anthony, playing in the Men's team.

"Anymore takers Steven?" shouted Jack from the back of the shop.

The shop door was ajar, and Steven turned his head abruptly to see who was shouting out.

"Oh, hi Jack. Yes, there's a few more since last week." He pointed to the form pinned to the noticeboard outside the shop.

"There's only one more training session for each of the teams so these late comers will have to step up to the mark."

"Have you got enough for both teams?" enquired Jack.

"Yeah, looks like it." Steven took the registration list down from the noticeboard and joined Jack in the shop. Putting the form down on the counter, he scanned the list.

"We could do with a few more on the girl's team, Jack."

"Let me see who's down already." Jack studied the list.

"Gee! Lorraine Thompson's put herself down; isn't she getting on a bit?"

"She's a relative newcomer to the village Jack, so I expect she just wants to get involved. I'll put her out on 'fine leg'. Anyway, I'll contact them all over the next couple of days and give them the run down for Saturday week. If you know of a couple more takers, can you let me know, Jack?"

"Sure Steven. I'll see what I can do."

It was cloudy but dry on the morning of the Annual Cricket Match. There was no movement in the village in the early hours apart from James McGregor bringing in his rubbish bin and mumbling to himself about no-one else being up and about. The evening before there had been excitement in the Shepherd's Arms as patrons placed their final bets on who would win, and shouts of 'let the best team win' as they raised their glasses for a toast.

Then, at seven o'clock on the dot, Steven Cosgrove in his tabletop truck with his two sons and a load full of trestle tables, bunting, cricket bats, stumps and the like, drove through the village.

The match was to be held on Braeside Oval, a large park big enough to hold such an event, on the edge of the village.

By eight o'clock three refreshment stalls had been erected and dozens of canned drinks, juices, tea, and coffee supplies were being arranged on the stalls. The game didn't start until ten o'clock but there was still much to do in preparation. Spectators began arriving with their fold-up chairs and picnic blankets; not only residents of Toveringham but some from surrounding villages. The event had indeed become quite a tradition over the years.

Jack and Rachel had donated several boxes of donuts, as was their custom, and the sausages for the Barbeque stall had been donated by Sean Blundle, the local butcher. Sean and his son James were preparing the barbeque when Hans Hoffner appeared.

"Well, you look a darn sight brighter than you did that day outside the docs."

Hans had encountered James doubled over outside the doctor's surgery the morning after the dinner/dance.

"Yeah, Mr Hoffner. It wasn't a very pleasant time, glad that's over. I don't suppose you'd like to help us here on the barbeque stand, would you? We could do with another pair of hands when it gets busy around lunchtime."

"Sure, no problem."

"If you come back about eleven o'clock to help me and Dad with the hot dogs that would be great. Thanks."

By lunchtime, when the makeshift scoreboard read 78 runs for the men, the crowds were hungry, and yes, it did get quite busy handing out hot dogs, drinks, donuts, and other delicious goodies. However, volunteers were there to help and there didn't seem to be any complaints from those attending the game.

The tradition was to let the youngest team member in to bat first. Adrian Cosgrove happened to be the one, he was eleven. After donning his protective headgear, he got into position ready to bat. His eyes focussed on the bowler at the other end of the pitch. Adrian and his family had always been interested in cricket, but he'd never played in a team.

The first ball, Adrian missed. The second ball, he swung his bat pretty hard but missed again. The third time, his bat finally made contact with the ball and sent it high in the air, out towards the boundary, where Lorraine Thompson had been placed. No-one knew much about Lorraine's past; after all she'd only been in the village for a year. Little did anyone know that she had been a keen sportswoman in her younger days and was still pretty fit for a fifty-one-year-old. She saw the ball coming straight for her and ran to meet it, bracing herself for the ball's impact. The rock-hard ball made contact with her hands but then bounced out of them. The crowd let out a loud "Aarrrgh" followed by cheers and clapping. Adrian managed to run the length of the pitch twice, by the time the ball got back to make contact with the stumps. Lorraine certainly showed off her skills that day, and so did Adrian. In fact, they both earned the titles of 'Woman of the Match' and 'Man of the Match', respectively.

The Shepherd's Arms was packed with patrons that evening. Karl and Michael had arrived back from their holiday and their visit to Cambridge a week earlier. Karl's suspicion proved correct, he and Michael were indeed half-brothers. It had shaken them both and the news had had an impact on their relationship. The atmosphere in the pub was one of celebration that evening as the men's team showed off their winner's trophy for the third year in a row.

"You wait, we'll beat you next year, mark my words!" shouted Sally Birchwell to the men at the bar. Michael smiled at her from behind the bar, trying with all his might to put on an interested face. At this very moment, he couldn't care less who won the wretched cricket match. All he knew was the life he'd planned with the man he loved was over.

Pamela and Janet were at their usual table with Constable Mark Fisher and Paul Bloomfield, discussing the game.

"I didn't know you played cricket Mark, let alone know how to umpire a cricket match. You seemed to know the rules very well," remarked Janet.

"Yes, I played a lot when I was training for the Police Force."

"Young Adrian Cosgrove did well, didn't he? Sending that ball right to the boundary."

"Yes, and what about Lorraine!" Janet butted in, "she's amazing for her age, don't you think? I hope I'm as fit as her when I get to her age."

Pamela looked sideways at her friend with a smirk on her face.

"What!" exclaimed Janet, "Don't you think I can be as fit as her?"

"Not if you keep eating those crisps!"

"With that, I think I'd better be going, got an early start tomorrow," said Mark, raising his glass to finish the last mouthful of lager.

"Yeah, me too," added Paul, "see you girls later."

Paul and Mark headed for the door leaving the girls to chat on their own.

"Did I tell you that I invited James to the game?" announced Pamela.

"No. What did he say?"

"Well, he declined my offer of course."

"That was very kind of you to offer to bring him. You're getting quite friendly with him, aren't you? Ever since you had him over for that cuppa. I'm really proud of you for doing that."

"Well, after that cuppa and the way he opened up to me about his daughter, I've been feeling sort of sorry for him, the poor thing. Did I tell you his daughter died of cancer?"

"Yes, you did. Pamela, have you ever thought that maybe he thinks of you as a substitute daughter?"

"What, me?"

"Yes, you know how you said he always seems to look out for you when you come home from work, and that. Well, he's probably yearning to have his daughter back, and you're the next best thing to that."

"I never thought of it like that."

"The poor guy. You know we should never really judge people. You never know what their story is, hey?"

Pamela took a sip of her lemon squash and sat pondering on Janet's last statement.

# CHAPTER 19

Tim Collins lay in bed staring at the ceiling of his bedroom. It was Sunday morning. The sun was already up, promising a warm day ahead. He could hear the church bells ringing from across the village green and put his hands over his ears to block the noise. The front door downstairs had just banged shut indicating his mum had just left for church. He hated Sundays. It meant that there was nothing much to do in this God forsaken village, not that he wanted to do much. Tim hadn't made any effort to make friends since their arrival and didn't want to get a job, at least not in this village. All he wanted to do was rewind the clock and go back to his old life in London. Tim kicked the bedcover off and sat up on the edge of the bed. The bottom drawer of his dresser was still open from last night when he hid the bottle of whiskey between his jumpers. The thought of what he'd done the night before gave him a sudden headache. He lay back down on his bed and tried to steer his thoughts to something more pleasant but failed.

Eventually the internet lured him into another world, and he sat at his computer for the rest of the day.

Meanwhile, Tim's mother knelt in the church pew deep in prayer, when she heard a voice say 'Jennifer'. She looked up, startled to see Father Morgan standing there. He'd just finished saying 'goodbye' to his parishioners outside and was on his way to the sacristy.

"Father John. Sorry, I didn't see you there."

"I didn't mean to interrupt, but I wondered how you were going with your son."

Tears began to well up in Jennifer's eyes as she tried to convey how worried she was about Tim. Father Morgan eventually took a seat next to Jennifer in the pew. He had no real answers for her, except to pray for guidance which they did together.

Natalie Hoffner struggled with her four-year-old son, Craig, as she entered Elam's shop. They were both dressed for the cold. Craig with a double-breasted, warm looking jacket and a handknitted beanie on his head; and Natalie with scarf and woollen gloves.

All of a sudden, a cold snap had descended on Toveringham, and everyone was feeling it. It was late October and Christmas seemed to be just around the corner.

"Hi Natalie. How is young Craig today?" Rachel greeted Natalie, noticing that Craig was playing up a bit.

"Oh, I'm fine, Rachel, but this one's been a bit naughty this morning" she said, giving her son a motherly glare of disapproval. "He doesn't want to keep his beanie on and it's freezing out there. He's just gotten over a cold, and I don't want him catching another one."

Rachel smiled at Craig, who had a sour look on his face.

"I've just dropped off Juliette at school and I was freezing standing at the gate."

"I know. I think we're in for a really cold winter. I've been meaning to ask you how Hans is going with the church bell ringing. I hear them ringing every Sunday morning as I'm having my cup of tea in bed."

Before Natalie had a chance to answer. Rachel continued, "Yes, I know what you're going to say, I should be going to church but it's the only day I have to lie in bed."

"You don't have to explain, Rachel. I don't blame you for wanting a lie in. And yes, Hans is doing well, thank you, he really enjoys it. He has to leave home earlier than us on Sundays and then I follow later with the children."

Natalie pulled out a handful of envelopes from her shopping basket.

"Rachel, I need to send these Christmas cards to Holland. Can you tell me how much they are, please?"

"You're rather early with these aren't you, Natalie?"

"I know, but Hans has been hounding me to get them off early this year seeing as last year we missed the cut off date. We've hardly finished with Easter and now they'll be getting their Christmas cards!"

"They're 80 pence each. That'll be six pounds 40 altogether."

Natalie pulled off her woollen gloves and placed them on the counter. She rummaged for her purse in her bag, keeping an eye at the same time on young Craig, who was eyeing up the Cadbury chocolate bars.

"Thanks Rachel." Natalie handed over a ten-pound note and quickly stuck the stamps on the envelopes before Craig got any ideas about wanting a chocolate bar.

"I'll post them outside?"

"Yes, please Natalie. The collection van will be coming later today. Oh! Don't forget your gloves." Rachel called out as Natalie turned to leave the shop, "You'll need them out there."

"Thanks Rachel."

As Natalie left the shop, she posted the Christmas cards in the red post-box built into the wall of Elam's shop. She was always fascinated by the little red post-box and thought it looked cute sitting in the wall.

# CHAPTER 20

Signs of the colder weather approaching were certainly in the air. The early morning frost lay sparkling on the village green, and leaves were falling leaving a blanket of brown crunching sounds under foot. Even the willow tree was beginning to lose its foliage. That didn't make any difference to Michael who had slipped out from the pub before breakfast. He now sat under the willow tree in his warm jacket buttoned up to his neck, looking out over the glistening grass.

There was only one thing on his mind: the future of his relationship with Karl.

They had been together for eight years and had planned on getting married in the not-too-distant future. How was that to happen now, with the knowledge that they were half-brothers? Michael wished with all his heart that Karl had never begun to investigate his family tree; then neither of them would be the wiser. He shivered in the cold morning air. He didn't really care about the cold, he just had to escape to think for a while.

Karl drew back the curtains of their bedroom and pulled on his dressing gown. The window overlooked The Green where he could see Michael sitting under the willow tree.

"*What on earth is he doing out there at this hour?*" Karl thought. He stared at the lonely figure on the seat. They had been through so much together over the years. The biggest hurdle of all, had been to convince their families to accept them as a gay couple. It had taken years for that to happen. Now, this latest hurdle was one that maybe neither could overcome. Karl remained at the window for some time thinking of the past eight years and wondering whether he should go to Michael.

Then he quickly tore off his dressing gown and put his puffer jacket over his pyjama top. He raced downstairs and pulling the main door shut he strolled over the road to where Michael was sitting. When he reached Michael, he stood for a while looking at him in silence. Michael looked up momentarily as if to acknowledge his presence while Karl sat down next to him.

"You must be freezing out here."

"Not really." Michael lied.

Karl was at a loss as to what to say next. The silence between them was like a dark cloud.

After a while Karl spoke.

"Look Michael, I just want to say that I wish to God I'd never tried to research my family tree. If I hadn't have done it, then things would have been a lot different."

"I don't blame you, Karl. All I want now is to know where we go from here?" He grabbed Karl's hand and clasped it in his.

It was Marge Saunders who happened to spot Karl and Michael under the willow tree that morning. Marge, of all people! She was sweeping the autumn leaves from her front porch. The boys hadn't noticed her, but she noticed them. As soon as she saw them, she quickly stopped sweeping and came inside to hide, spying behind her net curtains. She could tell something was up between them, by the way they were sitting, hunched over with their eyes on the ground as if they were deep in thought. Something was wrong. She just knew it. *Maybe they were in financial trouble with the pub; maybe their relationship was not going well? After all, gay people have break ups too,* she thought. Every conceivable dilemma went through her mind that morning. Poor Marge, she couldn't help herself. There always had to be something to gossip about.

That evening villagers had hardly finished dinner and settled in for the night, when already word had got out that Karl and Michael were having financial trouble with the pub. Marge had worked overtime in spreading the news via Elam's shop; outside the school gate that afternoon; and via the phone to Lorraine. She was adamant that it was financial trouble that they were going through. It could have been any number of things, but she settled on that one. Heaven forbid if word got back to Karl and Michael!

# CHAPTER 21

"What's that you're putting up there, Jack?" enquired Marge the next morning.

"Oh, it's a job opportunity, Marge. Fancy working for Father Morgan, do ya? Have a read of it."

Father Morgan had asked Jack to put a notice up on the shop noticeboard requesting applications for a part-time secretarial position at the presbytery. It read:

Secretarial Position (Part-time16 hours/week)
St Andrew's Catholic Parish
Applicant must have computer skills and a good knowledge of the Catholic ethos. Please address all applications with references to Father John Morgan, St Andrew's Catholic Parish, Templeman Road, Toveringham.

Marge smiled inwardly as she finished reading the notice.

*Humph. Sounds interesting. I could do that job*, she thought to herself.

"What can I do for you today, Marge?" asked Jack as he re-assembled some tins of baked beans on a shelf.

"I'll have some of your sliced ham please Jack, it's good for sandwiches. Oh, and a couple of tomatoes please, ripe ones, thanks."

"Is that enough ham Marge?" he held up some slices on greaseproof paper that he'd sliced on the machine.

"Yes, that's perfect, thank you. I'm having a few ladies over from the Women's Institute for morning tea tomorrow."

"Oh, that'll be nice" said Jack, picking out two ripe tomatoes from the basket he had on display.

A morning tea with the ladies from the Women's institute was a perfect opportunity for a good gossip, Jack thought to himself.

# CHAPTER 22

"How about this weekend, Brendan?" Paul Bloomfield, the pharmacist, was on the phone to his mate, Brendan, the local general practitioner.

"Let me check with Shirley in case she's got something planned. As far as I'm concerned though, it's okay."

"Let me know anyway. See you later."

"Okay, bye."

Brendan's wife, Shirley, hadn't planned anything special on the weekend. In fact, it was a great opportunity for her to pay a visit to her mother in Swindon.

Brendan and Paul had often gone fishing together, so it was scheduled for Sunday morning. They'd leave before dawn with fishing rods, bait, flasks of tea and sandwiches, and drive further out to the countryside for a day's fishing.

The air was crisp and fresh, but they had come prepared with jackets, scarves, and beanies. There was something wonderful about getting up before dawn in the dark and stillness of the country. There was also the opportunity for a good 'catchup' in the confines of the car.

"You know Brendan, you're lucky that Shirley lets you go fishing from time to time."

"Yeah, I am lucky I suppose. But she gets to mix with her friends too. When we got married, we agreed to let each other have time with our friends, as well as quality time with each other."

"That's what I would insist on if I ever met the right girl, which doesn't seem like it's going to happen now."

"Oh, don't be so negative Paul. You just never know what's around the corner. You know who I've always thought would be a good match for you."

"Who?"

"Helen Shrewsbury. You know, she's a teacher at the school."

"Helen Shrewsbury?" Paul stopped to think for a while. "Oh yeah, Helen. She comes into the pharmacy from time to time."

"She's widowed, isn't she?" Paul remarked.

"No, I don't think she's ever married. She's actually a very nice person, Paul." Brendan was trying his hardest to encourage Paul to come out of his 'bubble' and meet someone. After all, it had been several years since he had broken up with his fiancée. He had been devastated when it happened. Brendan had been a great support to him during that time. However, now his good mate thought it was high time Paul found someone to spend the rest of his life with.

"She came in the other week to buy some hair colour."

"Did she?"

"Yeah, the poor woman was struggling with her umbrella. The wind caught her skirt and lifted it up. I think she was a bit embarrassed by it."

"So, you remember her then?"

"Well, yes."

"Well, that's a good sign, that you noticed her and remembered her."

Brendan gave a cheeky smile as he glanced at his mate.

"Watch out for the sheep!" Paul shouted.

Brendan swerved just in the nick of time to miss a couple of sheep wandering onto the road.

"Phew! That was a close call." Brendan breathed a sigh of relief. "Now getting back to Helen Shrewsbury."

# CHAPTER 23

"Wooaah! Look at you all dressed up to the nines." Rachel blurted out as she saw Sean Blundle walk into the shop dressed rather smartly in a grey suit.

"Are you off to a funeral or something?"

"No!"

"What's with the suit then?"

"I've got to go into Ashbury for a meeting with the solicitor, you know, about the food poisoning."

"Oh, is it still going on?"

"Yeah. They've been dragging it out like crazy. I just wish they'd settle it once and for all and just pay us a bit of compensation. Every time I go in for a meeting, I have to leave James in charge of the shop. He can manage on his own, but I don't like doing it. There's a delivery from the abattoir today and I don't like him cutting up those carcasses on his own."

"Would you like Jack to go over and give James a hand?"

"Oh, that would be great if he could. It would be a load off my mind. Thanks so much."

"That's okay."

"What's okay?" interrupted Jack from behind the counter as he joined Rachel from out the back of the shop.

"You'll go and help James at the shop with the abattoir delivery, won't you?" Sean's a bit worried about how he'll cope."

"I've gotta go into Ashbury for a meeting." Sean added.

"Sure, that's okay. What time roughly?"

"I'll text you when I check with James, probably around lunchtime. Got to dash. Oh, I forgot, I came in for some chewing gum."

As Sean headed out of the shop, he passed Lorraine Thompson who was outside reading the notice about the secretarial position.

"Mornin' Lorraine."

"Oh, mornin' Sean. Nice day, isn't it?"

"Yes, it is."

Lorraine went back to reading the notice and making a mental note of the details. After buying a carton of milk and engaging in a brief chat with Rachel, she hurried home. She went straight into her study and grabbed a pen and paper from her desk, and quickly wrote down the details of the secretarial position. *She could do with a couple of days work to keep her mind active*, she thought. It was close to home, and she got on well with Father Morgan. The more she thought about it, the more she was determined to apply. Lorraine didn't waste any time. After putting the carton of milk away in the fridge and flicking the kettle on for a cup of tea, she sat down at her computer to put together her application.

Three weeks went by before Lorraine heard anything back from St Andrew's Presbytery. Although she saw Father Morgan every Sunday at Mass, nothing was mentioned about her application. However, it was one Friday when her mobile phone rang. She happened to be out in her garden in the winter sun tidying up some of her pot plants, when she heard it ring in the kitchen. Trying not to rush to the phone, as she was prone to doing (much to the disapproval of her daughter), she calmly removed her garden gloves. The phone had rung off by the time she reached the kitchen. She sat on her kitchen stool and tried to return the call.

"Hello, I've had a missed call from this number. It's Lorraine Thompson speaking."

"Lorraine! It's Father Morgan" came the reply.

Lorraine's face lit up. "Oh, Father Morgan. How are you?"

"I'm well, thank you. I'm ringing about your application for the secretarial position. I'd like you to come in for an interview."

"Of course. Thank you."

"Would Monday at ten o'clock suit?"

"Yes, that's fine. Thank you so much Father." Lorraine was smiling.

"See you on Monday then."

"Yes. Bye."

Lorraine was overjoyed. She'd actually got an interview! She hadn't been for an interview in years, she'd have to brush up on what to say and how to present herself. She couldn't wait to tell her daughter.

# CHAPTER 24

Pamela pressed James' front doorbell whilst juggling a dish of pasta bake in her other hand. It seemed to be a favourite of his and somehow Pamela had warmed to her elderly neighbour. She rang the doorbell again and waited. That's strange, she thought to herself. He'd normally have come to the door by now. She tried peering through the side window but couldn't see much, apart from James' cap and jacket hanging up on the hall stand. Pamela walked around the back of the house through the side passageway. The back door was open slightly. She called out to James several times, but no answer. Pamela felt a wave of trepidation as she crept apprehensively into the kitchen and placed the pasta bake onto the kitchen bench.

"James!" She called out again. "It's Pamela from next door."

Still no answer.

She pushed open the glass double doors that led to the lounge room. They were slightly ajar. There, on the carpet, lay James.

"Oh my God!" she shouted.

Pamela was shaking as she quickly checked if James was breathing. Thankfully he was breathing but he was unconscious. She quickly scanned the lounge and hallway for James' telephone and rang for an ambulance.

It seemed like an eternity before the paramedics arrived.

"Are you a relative?" one of them asked Pamela, as he knelt on the carpet beside James.

"No, I'm the next-door neighbour." Pamela felt her whole body shaking as she watched the paramedics assess James' condition. After about ten minutes they placed James onto a stretcher.

"Which hospital are you taking him to?" Pamela asked.

"Ashbury."

It was the next day that Pamela and Janet drove to Ashbury hospital to see James. Pamela was apprehensive about going on her own, so Janet went with her for support. Thankfully, James was conscious and had been placed in a ward with two other people. Apparently, he had suffered a stroke and his left side was slightly affected, but he could still speak. He had hit his head on his coffee table when he fell to the floor. So now he was sitting up in the hospital bed with a rather large dressing on his forehead.

"Well, you frightened the life out of me, James. I came to give you one of my pasta bakes and found you on the floor." Pamela tried to be light-hearted about the situation.

"Where's the pasta bake?" enquired James with a slight smile on his face.

"Well, I had to take it home to my place again. But I'll make you another one for when you come home, alright?"

"Good," he replied.

The reality was though, that James didn't go home. He had to be transferred to a nursing home as his condition didn't allow him to live on his own anymore. He was a bundle of nerves the day he entered the nursing home. Fortunately, Pamela was there to help him, and she vowed to visit him regularly, which he was pleased about. As James didn't have any relatives in the United Kingdom, Pamela had agreed to go through his belongings in his house to sort out what he'd need in the nursing home. It was a massive task which would take months; she was sure of that.

# CHAPTER 25

Sally Birchwell leaned slightly over the bar at the Shepherd's Arms and whispered to Michael, "Is the pub going okay?" Michael stopped in his tracks and stared at her.

"What do you mean?"

"You know. Are you in financial trouble? Sorry to ask, Michael, but I've heard some rumours."

Fortunately, the bar wasn't busy. Apart from Sally and James, there was only one other couple who were sitting at a table near the window. James made a face at Sally, disapproving of her rather inquisitive question.

"Rumours! What rumours?" Michael was horrified.

"Oh, you know how word gets around this village Michael. Only, if you are having trouble then don't hesitate to talk to us, if we can help, we will."

"Good grief Sally! I appreciate your concern, but you can go back to your source, whoever it was, and tell them they are wrong, and even if we were in strife, it's none of their bloody business!"

Michael was furious by this stage. On hearing a bit of the conversation, Karl joined Michael at his side.

"What's wrong?" he asked.

"Oh, there's rumours going around apparently that we're in financial strife."

"Rubbish!" Karl blurted out. "I bet it's that Marge Saunders again, she's a devil for starting rumours."

# CHAPTER 26

It had been a week since James had entered the nursing home and Pamela was getting ready to leave for work one morning. She lifted the heavy pile of library books she'd re-covered the evening before into the back seat of her car. Leaning on the top of the car door, her eyes couldn't help but focus on James' garden. She stood momentarily mesmerized by the wonderful job he'd done over the years to maintain his garden. Some weeds had now begun to poke through amongst his shrubs, and now tears began to blur her vision. Reaching into her skirt pocket for her handkerchief, memories of the day she got food poisoning came flooding back. How cranky she'd been with James and his busybody attitude; how unkind she'd been in ignoring him time after time. The tears flowed freely now as Pamela slumped into the driver's seat, overcome by emotion. James had become like a father figure to her. Her own father had died when she was very young, and her mother had remarried and now lived in Spain. Pamela had never experienced close at hand the twilight years of a parent. After a while she pulled herself together, started the car and reversed out of her driveway, noticing for the first time the crunching sound of her gravelled driveway under the car tyres. Life would be very different now that James didn't live next door. She'd actually miss him pottering in his garden every afternoon whilst waiting for her return from work.

Pamela and Janet had taken to meet in the pub for lunch on the colder days as winter set in. Today they treated themselves to a pub lunch. The weeping willow would still be there when the weather warmed up.

"There you go Pamela. A nice cup of tea."

"Thanks Janet. What did you order?"

"Two sausage rolls with sauce. Isn't that what you wanted?"

"Yes, that's fine, thanks."

"Now tell me, how's it all going? How are you coping?"

"Oh okay. I do miss seeing James every day standing in his front garden."

"Have you been to see him again?" Janet asked.

"Yeah, I went on Saturday. You should have seen his face when he saw me. He's a dear old chap. Oh, guess what? He said he wants to taste one of my pasta bakes again. I wonder if I'm allowed to take some in for him."

"You'll have to ask them." Janet suggested.

"Here we go ladies. Two sausage rolls with sauce and a plate of chips on the house."

"Thanks so much Michael!" the girls answered in unison.

"Come on, dig in. It'll take us a while to get through those chips and I've gotta be back by one thirty."

# CHAPTER 27

Monday morning came around all too quickly for Lorraine. She was hoping she'd prepared well enough for her job interview with Father Morgan however, she was quite nervous.

She straightened her navy, woollen skirt as she stood in front of her full-length mirror and leaned closer to check her lipstick. *Not too much, just enough to give a bit of colour,* she thought to herself. Her mind was full of all sorts of questions that Father Morgan might ask, and the answers she'd give. She checked the time on her bedside clock radio, *9.50 am. Just enough time to walk to the presbytery or should she drive? Just in case prying neighbourhood eyes will see her. Yes, it would be best to drive. Car keys; handbag; lock back door.*

"Okay I'm ready," she said.

"Good morning, Lorraine!" Father Morgan greeted her with a cheery smile. "Come on in, won't you?" he ushered Lorraine into what looked like his study. It was quite dark with heavy Victorian style furniture. His desk was huge, with a green, padded inlay on top and piles of papers arranged neatly on one side of the desk. Lorraine sat opposite him on an armchair that had seen better days.

After the usual pleasantries had been exchanged Father Morgan asked a few questions and then proceeded to explain the details of the position. The successful applicant would work one day per week commencing at eight-thirty in the morning and finishing at four o'clock and would be responsible mainly for the financial records and some general correspondence.

"Of course," he added, "confidentiality is of the utmost importance."

"Oh, I understand." Lorraine replied.

"Therefore, the business of the parish is not to be spoken about elsewhere."

Lorraine nodded in agreement.

"Do you have any questions, Lorraine?"

"No, not really Father Morgan. Oh, apart from when will the position commence?"

"As soon as possible. I'm in need of someone to start straightaway, my books are in a bit of a mess." He gave a bit of a chuckle. "However, I do have two other applicants to interview, so I'll be in touch soon."

"Thanks Father Morgan."

They shook hands and Lorraine left the interview feeling confident that she'd done the best she could.

# CHAPTER 28

Jennifer was just waking up when she heard the front door bang shut downstairs. It must be Tim going out. She glanced at the clock radio, trying to focus without her glasses. It was rather early. *What was he doing going out this early?* she thought. *The school bus wasn't due for another hour.*

Tim's behaviour had been more and more worrying lately. He would disappear at odd hours and hardly speak to her; only when it was necessary. He would lock himself in his room most evenings and Jennifer would often say 'goodnight' to him through the locked bedroom door, usually without any reply. Behind closed doors Tim would be drinking. It was the only comfort he knew to numb the loneliness and despair he was experiencing.

# CHAPTER 29

Christmas was fast approaching, and the spirit of the festive season was certainly spreading throughout Toveringham. Jack and Rachel Elam had ordered in Christmas hampers, Christmas crackers and all manner of decorations. The Shepherd's Arms had decorated the bar with lights and hanging paper bells. St Andrew's Church had placed the traditional outdoor nativity scene on display just inside their grounds, and many houses throughout the village had Christmas lights painstakingly placed around their front facades and gardens. Someone had even placed coloured tinsel around the trunk of the village green's weeping willow.

Lorraine Thompson was well and truly settled in her new position as secretary to Father Morgan, having been offered the job just two days after her interview. James McGregor was settling in well at the nursing home and looked forward each week to the regular visit from Pamela; and Michael and Karl were coming to terms with the fact that they may never be allowed to be married, but at least they were still together.

Paul Bloomfield had taken on board what his mate had said to him regarding Helen Shrewsbury, and the claim for compensation around the food poisoning fiasco was still a work in progress.

It was Christmas Eve and although it was threatening to snow, as the temperature dropped to below zero, some villagers were still out and about doing last minute shopping. Helen Shrewsbury was one of them.

She had just entered the pharmacy to pick up her prescription medication. Quickly closing the door to keep in the warm air, she expected to hear Paul's voice greeting her, as he always did. She looked around the shop but couldn't see any sign of Paul. Suddenly he appeared from behind the sunglasses stand wearing a thick, long and tangled white beard. Helen was startled to say the least.

"Is that you Paul?" she enquired.

"Oh, I'm sorry Helen" he mumbled through the beard, trying desperately to remove it. "I was just trying on my beard to see what it looks like."

"Well, take it from me, you look okay, but I much prefer the usual you, more handsome, wouldn't you say?" Paul was quite pleased at Helen's remark, though a little embarrassed.

"I take it you're going to be Father Christmas for the children tomorrow morning."

"Yes, they've asked me this year. Usually, Sean Blundle does it but as you know, he's got the flu. I have to practice my 'Ho, Ho, Ho's' before tomorrow morning; apparently you need to really disguise your real voice, so they tell me."

"Would you like to practice it now, and I can give you my honest opinion?"

Paul obliged with a mighty 'Ho, Ho, Ho!'.

"Oh, I think you'll make a great Father Christmas, Paul." Helen smiled.

# CHAPTER 30

The church bells of St Andrew's rang joyfully the next morning with the team of bell ringers, including Hans Hoffner, doing a fine job. The snow had arrived and was falling gently in soft flakes, leaving a white coating on everything it touched. The village of Toveringham looked as picturesque as any of the scenes one finds on a box of chocolates or a wall calendar.

The snow didn't deter the church goers. There seemed to be more worshippers than usual that morning, many with their families, and of course lots of children who were eager to see Father Christmas. The Toveringham tradition was such, that as soon as church had finished, the children would all rush over to the village green and wait for Father Christmas to arrive on a trailer pulled by a farm tractor. He would then throw chocolates to them as they all gathered excitedly around the trailer. Afterwards each child would be photographed with Father Christmas sitting under the weeping willow.

This morning however, as it was snowing, the treats would have to be given out in the parish hall. The hall was crowded and noisy by a quarter past ten, and word had got out that Father Christmas was on his way. Adults had congregated around the walls of the hall with the children jumping up and down with excitement in the middle. Eventually Father Christmas (alias Paul Bloomfield) arrived making an impressive entrance whilst ringing his bell and shouting 'Ho, Ho, Ho' to his heart's content.

"He makes a good Father Christmas, doesn't he Helen?" commented Dr Brendan Jones to Helen Shrewsbury, who just so happened to be standing next to him.

"Yes, he does rather." Helen replied.

"You just can't help yourself, can you Brendan." His wife, Shirley, who was standing on the other side of him, gave him a dig in the ribs. "Proper matchmaker, aren't you?" She whispered in his ear.

Father Christmas did a grand job entertaining the children and as they waved him off, gradually families dispersed, returning to their homes to enjoy turkey, brussel sprouts, plum pudding and put their feet up in the afternoon to watch the Christmas message from the Queen.

"We should really do something about this hall," commented Marge Saunders to Rachel Elam as they pulled the door of the parish hall shut.

"We are, didn't you hear? The compensation has come through and they're going to renovate the hall with the money."

A look of utter surprise spread over Marge's face.

"Oh, oh really? Oh, of course" she stammered.

*How come I didn't know about this*, she thought to herself. *How dare no-one inform me!*

Rachel gave a cheeky smirk as Marge turned to walk away flinging her knitted pink and grey scarf, with an air of disgust, over her shoulder.

# CHAPTER 31

Snow had fallen steadily throughout Christmas Day covering the entire village with a glistening white powder. By Boxing Day afternoon, the snow had stopped falling and a few children were out on the village green throwing snowballs at each other and making snowmen.

In the Shepherd's Arms, Paul and Brendan as well as Brendan's wife Shirley were sitting at a table near the open fire enjoying a drink.

"I think you should be Father Christmas every year, Paul. You did a terrific job." Shirley announced.

"Actually, I quite enjoyed it, though the suit was a bit hot and the beard very itchy!" they all had a good chuckle.

"Do you fancy having dinner here tonight?" Brendan asked.

"Yeah, why not. I've got nothing to go home to," added Paul.

"Well, that could change if you allowed it to happen, you know."

"Oh, here we go again!" Paul was beginning to get fed up hearing the same thing over and over.

"Well, why don't you try asking her out," Shirley butted in, "the worst that can happen is she'll say 'no'."

Just then Karl came around to wipe down the table next to them.

"Did everyone have a good Christmas, then?" he asked, trying to be sociable.

"Yes, thanks Karl," they all replied.

"By the way, if anyone's interested in staying in for dinner, I can recommend the braised beef in butter with mushrooms."

"That sounds good Karl" responded Brendan, "what do you reckon everyone? Three braised beef?"

The three were enjoying their meal when Shirley suddenly blurted out, "Oh wow! Don't turn around but guess who's just walked in?"

Paul and Brendan stopped eating and stared at Shirley without turning around. "Who is it?" Brendan asked, staring at his wife.

"It's Helen," she whispered.

"Oh really!" Brendan's eyes lit up and he immediately turned around to look.

Shirley kicked her husband under the table. "Honestly Brendan, anyone would think you're after her for yourself and not for Paul!"

"Sshhh! I'm not after her, it's you guys that are pushing me."

Within a couple of minutes, Brendan announced, "Quiet! She's coming over."

"Hello everyone!" Helen was carrying a small bottle of rum, encased in a brown paper bag, which she'd just bought at the bar.

"You must think I'm on the booze, but this is for culinary purposes," she explained.

"We weren't thinking anything of the sort, Helen. Here come and join us." Brendan pulled out the vacant chair next to him.

"Oh, I don't want to disturb you, you're eating."

"Well, we've almost finished, haven't we guys?

"I'll join you for a little while, if that's okay?"

"What are you using the rum for, Helen?" Shirley asked.

"Oh, I'm making a Christmas cake. It sounds silly because Christmas is over, but you see I never seem to have the time to make one before Christmas, so I've got into the habit of making one every year on Boxing Day. I started preparing it this morning but then realised I didn't have any rum, so here I am."

"What are you doing on New Year's Eve, Helen? Got any plans?" Brendan didn't mince his words and got straight to the point. Paul could feel himself blushing because he knew what was coming next.

"Well, I always spend it at home really, an early night and all that."

"You're welcome to join me and Shirley at our place. We're just having drinks and a light supper. You could bring some of your Christmas cake, if you like?"

"Thank you, that's nice of you to invite me."

Paul couldn't believe his ears! His mate was very cunning indeed to be inviting Helen to drinks to bring in the New Year. He just wanted to throw the pair together. Brendan knew that Paul would come over on New Year's Eve as well. It was tradition. He always did.

# CHAPTER 32

Brendan and Shirley Jones lived behind the surgery in a rather modern part of the old house which had been renovated to their taste. They didn't have children so the house was always immaculately clean and tidy. To access the house, guests had to go down a side passageway which led to double doors with a large Christmas wreath hanging from the door knocker.

Helen arrived on New Year's Eve carrying a plate of her recently baked Christmas cake. She knocked on the door and waited for Brendan or Shirley to answer. To her surprise it was Paul that answered the door.

"Oh, hello Paul," she looked a bit surprised, as was Paul, who was convinced that Helen wouldn't accept Brendan's invitation.

"Come in," he said politely.

There were more guests than Helen expected. She was not the type to socialise in large numbers, especially amongst people she didn't know. However, there was Paul to talk to, she thought to herself, and she was happy to get to know him.

"Hello Helen! Glad you could come," Brendan greeted her with a smile and offered to take her coat once she was inside.

"Let me guess, that must be your Christmas cake? Can I take it from you?

Can I get you a drink, Helen?"

"Yes, something soft please, maybe an orange juice, if you have some."

Brendan turned to go and organise Helen's drink. He left Paul standing there with Helen, hoping that they would start a conversation.

"They've got a lovely home, Brendan and Shirley, don't you think."

"Yes, it's been renovated throughout."

There was a few seconds of silence. Then …

"Um … how did your Christmas cake turn out?"

"Well, good! I think, I brought some tonight."

Paul smiled politely. Conversation was quite strained at first, but by the end of the evening Paul and Helen were sitting, side by side on the lounge, deep in conversation. Helen left for home well before midnight which was much to Paul's relief. He was envisaging what he would do at midnight when everyone hugged and kissed each other. *They did get on well*, he thought, *but it would have been a bit awkward.*

When all the guests had returned to their homes and the New Year was well and truly in, Brendan and Shirley decided to leave the mess until the morning. However, not without a final few words on how well it all went, and especially how well Paul and Helen seemed to get on.

"Didn't they go well together? They were both talking for ages. I'd love to know what they were talking about." Brendan said with delight in his eyes.

"Oh honestly! Now look Brendan, you've done your bit, it's now up to them, okay?" Shirley closed the subject before kissing her husband and turning off her bedside light.

# CHAPTER 33

The winter had been bitterly cold, but now the weather was warming up and Spring was on its way. Crocuses and snowdrops were beginning to make an appearance through the frozen earth. Even the weeping willow was showing signs of new life with tiny yellow flowers emerging on its branches.

Janet and Pamela were enjoying their usual lunch together under the willow and trying to soak up the sun whilst it was out, when they saw Jennifer Collins rush out of the school gate in what seemed like a frantic hurry.

She seemed like she was heading home.

"Wow! Do you think she's alright?" asked Pamela with a concerned look on her face.

"I don't think so. Something must be wrong. Gee! She looks like she's in a real hurry."

"I wonder what it is."

As Jennifer drew closer to home, she could see her neighbour standing near her front gate waiting for her. She ran the last few metres to her gate.

"Where is he?" she cried out, almost out of breath.

Her neighbour pointed, "Inside."

Jennifer ran through her open front door to find Tim sitting at the kitchen table with a glass of whiskey in his hand.

"Hello Mother! Cheers!" he raised his glass to her.

Jennifer stared at her son, lost for words. She couldn't believe this was her Tim, he was as drunk as anything. She finally plucked up courage and with anger growing inside her she said, "Where did you get that drink?"

"Why? Would you like some, Mother dearest?"

She repeated herself, "Where did you get that drink?"

"It's hiding in my jumper drawer Mummy dearest. But if you want some, you'll have to be quick as it's nearly all gone," Tim laughed a hideous laugh that turned Jennifer's stomach. At that moment, she didn't know how she felt as a mixture of anger, fear and anxiety were all rolled into one big knot in her stomach.

Outside, her neighbour was still standing by their gate waiting.

"Thanks for ringing me, John. I really appreciate it."

"I was a bit worried when Tim came out and started shouting at Beryl," John explained.

"She was in the front garden, you see. We could both see he was drunk. That's when I thought it best to ring you."

"I'm very grateful John. Is Beryl okay?"

"Yes, she's fine."

"You've got your hands full there, my dear. Let us know if we can do anything."

"Thank you, John. If you don't mind just keeping this to yourself, please?"

Jennifer had to return to school, it was her lunchbreak, but she didn't feel at all like eating. Her mind was not on her class that afternoon. All she could think of was Tim and the uncertain times ahead.

# CHAPTER 34

Pamela arrived at the nursing home for her regular visit with James. It happened to be his 88th birthday so she was laden with a box of chocolates, bunch of mixed flowers and a book by his favourite author, Agatha Christie.

Now that James' eyesight was deteriorating, Pamela had begun reading to him. He thoroughly enjoyed listening to the stories and often said to her, "you read so well, my dear, with such wonderful expression." Her face would light up when hearing that, and she found herself grateful for the opportunity to bring some joy into James' life.

A member of staff passed her in the corridor and stopped to admire the flowers Pamela was carrying.

"Oh, James will be pleased to see you. He keeps reminding us that it's his birthday today, bless him. We'll let you settle with him for a while and then we'll bring in the birthday cake. He's in the Common Room."

James' face lit up when everyone sang 'Happy Birthday' to him. Pamela had never seen him smile so much as he did that day, his rotten teeth once more coming out of hibernation! There was no time for reading today as the emphasis was on the birthday celebration and eating cake! At the end of Pamela's visit he confided in her that this was the first time since his daughter had died that he'd had a birthday cake. Pamela gave him a goodbye hug and left James sitting contentedly in an armchair with flowers, chocolates and birthday cards surrounding him.

Michael and Karl were up early attending to a six o'clock delivery from the brewery. They were helping offload the barrels into the pub's cellar when Karl stopped momentarily, with his hands on his hips, for a rest. He looked over to the village green and spotted someone out walking.

"Hey Michael, isn't that the young guy from the thatched cottage? He's up early, isn't he?"

"Oh yeah, I think it is. Doesn't he go to school in Ashbury?"

"Yeah. I wonder what he's doing at this hour, it's a bit early to catch the school bus, don't you think?"

"Come on Karl. Stop gawking at him and come and help me with this."

The fact was, Tim Collins was out early again, dressed in his school uniform, but much too early to catch the school bus. Where was he going at this hour?

# CHAPTER 35

Paul Bloomfield had learnt from his past experiences with women that trust is extremely important in any relationship. When his fiancée had called their wedding off several years ago, it had caused Paul to tread very carefully with the opposite sex. The truth was he didn't seem to trust any woman that he'd encountered since then. He would put up walls, not allowing anyone to get to know the real Paul. Somehow though, since New Year's Eve, he hadn't been able to get Helen off his mind. He sighed as he re-stocked the shelf with throat lozenges and cough suppressants. His mind wandered back and forth, from throat lozenges to Helen, and back to cough suppressants. He'd never felt this way about anyone before. Why was this so different? He turned around and found himself pausing to check his reflection in the sunglasses mirror at the end of the counter. *Was he too old now for any woman, now that he had greying hair and a somewhat sagging neck? Was fifty-eight too old to be dating women?*

Just then the pharmacy door flung open and jolted Paul out of his dream-like state. It was Sally Birchwell.

"Mornin' Paul. I hope I didn't disturb you." Sally had noticed Paul staring at himself in the mirror as she walked past the pharmacy window.

"Er, mornin' Sally. How are you?" he decided to ignore her comment about disturbing him, it was just easier that way.

Meanwhile, at No.3, Park View Lane, Helen Shrewsbury was tidying her snug, arranging cushions on the sofa, re-arranging ornaments and generally forcing herself to be busy. She'd been up since the crack of dawn, not being able to sleep, and she wondered how she would now fill in the day. Every day, since New Year's Eve, her mind had been filled with thoughts of Paul. Helen was so worried about the thought of getting to like him that for weeks now she had purposefully stayed away from the pharmacy. Instead of filling her scripts and buying her hair colour from the pharmacy, she went into Ashbury to buy what she needed.

Helen sat for a while in her armchair as she was tired of her mind being constantly consumed by thoughts of Paul. Slowly her mind drifted back to the time when she was fresh out of teacher's college and in her first appointment as a Reception teacher in a small school in Sussex. It was there that she met and fell in love with Stuart, a colleague who was teaching fifth grade. They had been going out for almost two years and Helen had high hopes for their future together, when suddenly Stuart dropped a bombshell; he had met another woman. Helen had been heartbroken, and it took her many months to come to terms with the fact that her dreams for their future together had been shattered. Boyfriends had come and gone over the years, but none had fitted the bill like Stuart had … until now.

Brendan had left the subject of Helen alone for a few months (on instructions from his wife, Shirley) and didn't mention it to Paul whenever they were together. It actually gave Paul time to really reflect on the future, whether it be with Helen or not.

# CHAPTER 36

The kettle on the hob whistled madly shooting steam from its spout as it came to the boil. Lorraine rushed to the kitchen to retrieve it. She was running late for work, having slept through the alarm. *No time for even a cup of tea*, she thought as she checked the kitchen clock. Although Father Morgan was quite relaxed when it came to punctuality, she didn't want to make a bad impression this early in the piece.

Lorraine grabbed her jacket from the hall stand and headed out of the door. She walked briskly to the presbytery, trying not to focus on how hungry she was, having not had time for breakfast. She had been given a key to the presbytery by Father Morgan, which made it easy for her to come and go.

"Morning Father Morgan," she called out as she opened the front door.

"Morning Lorraine. I'm in the kitchen."

"How are you Father?" she enquired walking through to the kitchen.

"I'm well, thank you. Would you like a cuppa? I've just boiled the kettle."

"Oh, that would be lovely. I didn't have time for one this morning. In fact, I've got a confession to make, I slept in, right through the alarm."

"Oh really. I hope the work is not tiring you out too much."

"Oh no, not at all. I'm really enjoying it. Really I am."

"That's good. I must say I'm happy with the way it's working out. It certainly is a big help to me; especially that you are doing the bookkeeping."

Lorraine smiled as she made herself a cup of decaffeinated coffee and helped herself to a biscuit from the tin in the cupboard.

"Well, I'd better get started," she said as she made her way towards her office. It was a small room in the front of the presbytery. It could have been a living room in days gone by. Father Morgan had placed in it a desk with computer and office chair, and filled it up with an armchair, tall potted plant and a bookcase which held the registers of the parish as well as numerous books on the theology of the church. The large bay window overlooked the front garden, so Lorraine was able to see anyone coming up to the front door.

It was a pleasant room and Father Morgan had gone to great lengths to make it as comfortable as possible for his new secretary.

It was Tuesday and Father Morgan had a couple of appointments to attend to in the morning, as well as an afternoon meeting at the school.

Lorraine settled down at her desk and read the handwritten note from Father Morgan, detailing his movements for the day. She sipped on her coffee whilst reading the note. He would always finish the note by writing, '*Have a pleasant day*', which she felt was rather nice.

Father Morgan had been standing in the doorway of her office for a few seconds before Lorraine noticed him. She lifted her head up from the register she was working on.

"Oh, sorry Father. I didn't see you there."

"That's okay, I could see you were busy. I'm off now to the nursing home for anointing. I should be back around eleven o'clock.

Lorraine watched Father Morgan make his way out of the door towards his car parked in the street. He was a tall, slim man with square shoulders but slightly bent over these days. His hair, what was left of it, was almost totally grey. Lorraine guessed that he was probably in his early seventies. He still had a slight spring in his step; there was certainly no need for a walking stick just yet. She watched him closely as he got into his car and drove off. How fortunate she was to be working for such a lovely priest.

The morning passed quickly, and hunger pangs reminded her that she hadn't eaten anything apart from a biscuit with the coffee. Father Morgan hadn't yet returned from the nursing home, so she decided to go out and grab a sandwich from Elam's shop.

"Hello Lorraine," Rachel greeted her as she entered the shop, "how are you?"

"I'm well thanks. Just on my lunchbreak and wondered if you could make me a ham, cheese and tomato sandwich."

"Sure. How's it all going working for Father Morgan?"

"Really well. He's such a nice, easy-going man to work for."

"Well, I'm glad you got the job and not Marge. Oh heavens! Maybe I shouldn't have said that!"

"That's okay Rachel. I know she applied for it, she told me. The thing is I didn't tell her that I was applying for it. Anyway, she found out I got the job of course and ever since then she's been rather cool towards me."

"Don't worry, she'll get over it."

Rachel sliced the tomato to put onto Lorraine's sandwich, pressed a slice of buttered bread on top before cutting the sandwich into two triangles. She then placed the sandwich into a brown paper bag, "That's one pound fifty please Lorraine. You have a good afternoon."

"You too. See you later."

Lorraine had just finished her sandwich when she heard Father Morgan's key go in the door. She heard him talking to someone as he entered the presbytery. The woman's voice was not one she recognised. He went straight into the kitchen where he introduced his visitor, Jennifer Collins, to Lorraine. He then asked Lorraine to hold any phone calls for him, and he and Jennifer retreated behind the closed door of his study.

Lorraine hadn't met Jennifer before, but she knew the name 'Collins' and suspected she was the mother of Tim Collins, whom Marge always mentioned.

Marge had her own suspicions about the boy; that he seemed, in her own words 'strange'. He would never talk to anyone; he'd been seen roaming the streets of Ashbury early some mornings, and Marge had formed the conclusion that he was on drugs. Lorraine had tried to dismiss everything that Marge had to say about the boy; after all, it was none of their business.

After about half an hour, Father Morgan and Jennifer emerged from the study and walked to the front door. "Let me know how you go, Jennifer," he said as he saw her out.

"I will. Thank you, Father," came her reply.

"Phew! What a day!" Father Morgan flopped into the armchair that had its home in Lorraine's office.

"You have been rather busy today, haven't you?" Lorraine remarked. "Can I make you a cuppa?"

"That would be lovely. Thanks Lorraine."

So, the two of them spent the remainder of the working day sipping tea and talking about life in a parish. Lorraine came away thinking about the busy life of a priest and how she had come to realise just how hectic and varied their day can be.

# CHAPTER 37

Easter was always a pleasant time of the year in Toveringham. Spring was in full swing; the daffodils and bluebells were nodding their yellow and blue heads in the cool breeze. The weeping willow was again sweeping the duck pond with its long, slender branches, and the sun would hopefully be shining. Many of the women in the village would be shopping for a new hat to wear at church on Easter Sunday. One of those women was Rachel Elam.

"What do you think, Jack? Do you like it?" Rachel asked her husband one morning whilst admiring herself in the bedroom mirror.

"Like what?"

"The hat of course."

"Oh, I see. What's that in aid of? Have we got a wedding to go to?"

"Of course not, silly. It's for Easter Sunday, for church."

"Church! But we never go to church."

"Well, we are this year, dear."

"Whatever for? You've never wanted to go before."

"Well, I do this year. All the women from the Women's Institute are going and I thought that seeing we are a prominent establishment in the village, that we should be seen to be going to church."

"You've been talking to someone, haven't you?" Jack was sceptical of Rachel's motives.

"I just think we should go and give thanks for everything that we have. Now, what are you going to wear to church?" Rachel turned to open Jack's side of the wardrobe and pulled out a suit.

"What about your dark grey suit. It goes rather well with the pink colours in my hat, don't you think?"

"That's what I wear to funerals!"

"Well not this time Jack Elam. You'll be wearing it on Easter Sunday."

The sun was indeed shining on Easter Sunday morning and St Andrew's church bells were ringing as villagers and visitors flocked to the Easter service. One could hardly see Father Morgan for all the colourful Easter hats that were proudly worn by many women in the congregation. Everything from feathers, ribbons, flowers, eggs, chicks, satin and netting of every colour and description adorned the hairpieces. It was a sight to behold! After the service the village green became the focus for an Easter egg hunt.

Jack and Rachel Elam were standing near the church gate watching the children all rush over to the village green when Paul Bloomfield came up to them.

"You're looking quite dapper in your suit, Jack."

"Oh, hello Paul, I didn't see you there. Don't mention the suit, I got conned into wearing it," Jack threw a sour look towards Rachel as he said it.

"Oh dear," Paul gave a chuckle and then changed the subject.

"I hear they're starting renovations on the hall after Easter."

"Yes, Sean was telling me that the tradesmen are coming on Tuesday. I guess it won't be so quiet around here with all that going on."

"Mmmm, anyway, it's long overdue."

Just as Paul said that he spotted Helen in the distance. She had her back towards them, with her new hat camouflaging her appearance. As she turned around to speak to someone, Paul noticed her. He stared at her for some time. Jack and Rachel, who were still standing next to him, sensed he was otherwise occupied after they got no reply to a question they put to him.

"Paul!"

"Oh sorry! What was that?"

"I said does Doc Brendan normally come to church on Easter Sunday?"

"Oh yes, normally. However, they've gone away for the long weekend. Would you excuse me for a second," Paul gave his apologies with some feeble excuse so he could leave the discussion and go to wish Helen a 'Happy Easter'.

He weaved his way towards Helen, trying not to look like he was making a 'bee line' for her.

"Happy Easter Helen!"

"Oh, hello Paul. Happy Easter to you too."

"I must say your Easter hat is rather stunning."

"Thank you. I don't normally wear a hat but today's the exception."

"Well, it suits you," Paul nodded with a smile.

"Have you been well?" Helen enquired.

"Yes, not too bad. What about you?"

"Yes, fine thanks."

Paul was dying to say he'd missed seeing her come into the pharmacy but didn't think it was appropriate.

There was so much he longed to tell her but he couldn't bring himself to do it.

What was happening to him? Why did he suddenly feel this way?

Their initial encounter on New Year's Eve at Brendan and Shirley's had been wonderful, but then everything had come to a standstill. He was glad that Brendan and Shirley were away for the weekend and not now breathing down his neck as he stood in front of Helen trying to make conversation.

# CHAPTER 38

It was market day and the village woke up to drizzling rain. However, that didn't deter stallholders; market day went ahead come rain, hail or shine. It would take more than a bit of rain to stop market day in Toveringham. Anyway, the forecast was for showers to ease by the afternoon.

Pamela Yates was up early doing her weekly wash. She would have to put her clothes into the tumble drier due to the rain outside. She hadn't been to the weekly market for a while but felt like paying it a visit before she went to see James in the nursing home. She glanced at James' front garden as she got into her car. It was looking good, she thought to herself. She had managed to spend some time tending to the weeds and generally maintaining it, but felt it needed a bit more colour. She had promised James she would look after his garden, having spent many weekends going through his belongings in his house and transferring most of what he needed to his room in the nursing home. Anyway, maybe she could find some new plants at the market to bring some colour into the garden. After an enjoyable hour at the market, she came home laden with hyacinth and tulip bulbs, as well as some home-made apple jelly (which she loved), and some decorative coat hangers (which she could put away for Christmas presents). Before heading off to the nursing home, she made herself a sandwich and then took a photo of James' front garden with her mobile phone.

James' face lit up when he saw her politely knock on the door of his room. It was just after lunch, and he was watching television. She noticed his lunch tray on the table in his room with a half-eaten meal left on the plate.

"Hello James," Pamela greeted him with her usual happy tone.

"My word you look pretty in that dress," he said as she came up closer to give him a kiss on the cheek. Pamela was wearing a brightly coloured floral dress that was eye-catching.

"I call it my Spring dress," she said, "it reminds me of Spring; you know, tulips and daffodils."

"Yes, I see," James nodded.

"Talking about Spring flowers; have a look at this," Pamela pulled out her mobile phone from her handbag and showed James the photo she'd taken that morning. "Here's your front garden James, as it looks now. However, this morning I bought some hyacinth and tulip bulbs from the market. I thought I'd plant them this weekend and they should be ready for next Spring.

"Are you sure that's my garden?" questioned James.

"Yes, of course it is. I took the photo this morning with my mobile."

"What, with that?"

"Yes, that's how you do it these days, James."

"Oh my! Things have changed, haven't they?" he smiled.

"People don't use cameras much these days, only mobile phones. Anyway, how are you?"

Pamela made herself comfortable in the visitor's chair next to the window.

"Oh, I'm okay," he said with a rather blank expression on his face.

"Are you eating well? I noticed you've left some of your meal."

"Oh, I don't like broccoli, and they always give me too much."

"I see." Pamela felt that James was making excuses for not eating all his meal.

She stayed a good while talking to James about what was happening in the village – the childrens' Easter egg hunt; the hall renovations and how many chocolate eggs she had devoured over Easter!

By the time she left the nursing home the rain had stopped, and the sun was out, as predicted. On the way out she stopped one of the staff.

"Er, excuse me. I wonder if you can help me. I'm a friend of James McGregor."

"Oh yes … you're Pamela, aren't you? James often talks about you."

Pamela smiled inwardly in the knowledge that she was important enough in James' life for him to talk about her.

"Well, I've noticed that he doesn't seem to be finishing his meals. Is that normal for someone his age?"

"Yes, sometimes the appetite does diminish slightly as one gets older. However, I'll have a word with our dietician regarding James' diet and get back to you."

Pamela was grateful and walked away from the nursing home content that she'd aired her concern with a member of staff. She stopped at the supermarket on the way home to pick up some cream, which was needed for the dinner she'd planned for that evening. She was having Janet over, and spaghetti carbonara was on the menu.

Back in the village, Paul Bloomfield was getting ready to close the pharmacy for the day. He went to the door to turn the sign to CLOSED and noticed some stallholders across the road were beginning to pack up. He lingered for a moment watching them, then noticed Helen was outside the leather bag stall admiring a handbag. He froze. The moment had come; *it was now or never*, he thought. Butterflies began to form in his stomach, and he realised that there would only be one of two possible outcomes from what was to transpire. He would either return to the pharmacy after going to speak to Helen; elated, or dejected! He grabbed his keys and pulled the pharmacy door shut behind him, and without wavering he strode purposefully across to where Helen was standing.

"Hello Helen," he said confidently.

She turned around on hearing his voice, "Oh hello Paul. I didn't see you there. I'm just wondering whether to buy this bag or not."

He ignored her reference to the bag and went 'in for the kill'.

"Helen, I was wondering if you'd like to accompany me to a theatre production of 'Pirates of Penzance' next Saturday evening."

The words sprang out of his mouth in such a flurry, without any pause for a breath. He couldn't believe he'd done it. Helen stood for a moment as if in a trance and then said, "I'd love to Paul. I love the theatre."

That was music to his ears. He could feel his body physically relax and hoped it wasn't noticeable to Helen. At last, he'd done it! What a relief!

What should he say next? The words didn't seem to come. Helen came to the rescue by asking what time she should be ready and if they were going in his car. She concluded by saying, "I'll look forward to it," and smiled graciously.

"Good," was all Paul could say and then added, "Oh by the way, it's a nice bag."

# CHAPTER 39

That evening Pamela and Janet sat down to a delicious meal.

"You certainly have a flair for Italian cuisine," remarked Janet twirling the spaghetti around her fork.

"Do you think so?"

"Yes, what with your famous pasta bake that James likes so much and now the carbonara."

"Well, make sure you make room for dessert; there's cheesecake to come."

"Yum!"

"How is James, by the way?" Janet enquired.

"I went to see him today actually. He's okay, though I noticed he hadn't been finishing his meals, so I spoke to a member of staff about it. They said they'd check on it."

"You know the elderly do tend to eat less as they get older."

"Yeah, that's what the staff member said."

"You know you're very good to go and see him as often as you do."

"Well Janet, he's got no other living relative here to visit him. Besides I do enjoy his company."

"Wow! That's a turnaround from a year or so ago!"

"Yeah, I know. Isn't it strange how our lives change?"

# CHAPTER 40

Life had certainly changed for Jennifer Collins and not necessarily for the better. She stood at her kitchen sink washing the dishes from dinner. Her usual swiftness in tackling the kitchen chores was now replaced by slower movements as she reflected on her life. She stared out of the window with her hands immersed in the soap suds in the sink. The evening light was dimming as the sun slowly disappeared beyond the back hedge. That was just how she felt; as if the sun was going down on her life. Her move to the country was meant to be a new beginning after her divorce.

She thought it was the best thing for her and Tim, but now she felt as if it had been a huge mistake. This wasn't peaceful, country living. This was a nightmare! Yes, she had a good job at the school, which she liked, but she also had a son who wouldn't communicate with her and had turned to drink. Heaven knows how he got hold of it, and she didn't want to know. Father Morgan had been of some support, but he didn't have all the answers. Tim's school suggested counselling, but how can you get someone to counselling who wouldn't even listen to you? Most of his time at home was spent up in his bedroom, locked away from the world. This wasn't any life for him or for her. As she stared into the darkness the thought flashed through her mind of moving back to London. How absurd was that? They had only just arrived! It would be an upheaval again and the financial burden of another move would be crippling.

# CHAPTER 41

The following weekend Pamela was in James' garden planting the bulbs she had bought from the market, when young Adrian Cosgrove rode by on his bike. Seeing Pamela in James' garden he slowed down and stopped by the gate.

"Morning' Miss Yates," (all the children in the village referred to her as Miss Yates as she was the local librarian). "Did you know you're in the wrong garden?" he said with a cheeky smile.

"Yes, I know Adrian," she said, slowly straightening up.

"I'm planting some tulips for James. He's gone to live in a nursing home in Ashbury. I'm looking after his garden for him."

"Oh, I see. Is he okay?"

"Well yes, but he won't be coming back here to live unfortunately. It happens to all of us Adrian, we get older and sometimes we're unable to look after ourselves, so someone has to do it for us," she said this with a somewhat melancholy tone in her voice.

"Oh, I'm sorry to hear that," Adrian said.

"I'll tell James you were asking after him when I go and see him."

"Yeah, okay and tell him I said my mum's cauliflower cheese is just as good as ever. He'll know what you mean."

"Okay, I will."

"See ya, Miss Yates."

"Bye Adrian."

# CHAPTER 42

Paul opened the passenger door of his car for Helen. She was dressed very appropriately in a pale green knitted top with matching coloured skirt, and he recognised the handbag hanging from her shoulder; the one she was admiring at the market.

"I see you bought the handbag," he said as he got into the driver's seat.

"Oh yes. Do you like it?"

"Yes, it suits you."

She was happy with the compliment.

The theatre production was brilliantly staged, although Paul couldn't really comment on it as his thoughts were elsewhere. For the duration of the performance, he looked straight ahead at the stage but glanced at Helen through the corner of his eye, checking to see if she was still there and that he wasn't just imagining it.

They finished the evening with a cup of hot chocolate at a nearby café. Helen opened up about her love of theatre and how she had been involved in several productions as a teenager. Paul was mesmerized and didn't want the evening to end. Driving home, he could feel himself getting more nervous as they drew closer to Helen's house with the thought of what to do to end the night. *What was appropriate on a first date? A kiss on the cheek? A hug? A mere 'thank you'? Definitely not a kiss on the lips – not this early in the piece – surely!*

They talked for a while, after pulling up outside Helen's gate and then Helen said, "Well, I guess I must be off, it's getting a bit late. Thank you, Paul, for a really lovely evening, I've really enjoyed it."

"Yes, so have I. Thank you, Helen." Then boldly and without hesitation, Helen said, "We must do it again some time."

"Yes definitely," Paul replied and placed his hand on hers giving it a gentle squeeze.

Thinking the nervous part was all over, he then realised, being a gentleman, that he'd have to walk her to her front door. *What in heaven's name was he going to do there?* Fortunately, Helen took control of the situation at the door, and on saying 'goodbye' she leaned forward to give Paul a kiss on the cheek.

As he drove off, both he and Helen were on 'cloud nine' as they waved goodbye to each other. At long last the ice had been broken!

# CHAPTER 43

"Hey Michael. What do you reckon about Paul Bloomfield and Helen?" Karl motioned his head towards the window where Helen and Paul were sitting together.

"They've been coming in more often recently. Have you noticed?"

"Yeah, I've noticed."

"Do you think there's a romance blooming? Ha, ha! Do you get it? Bloomfield ... Blooming!"

"Yes, I get it. Very funny. You never were any good at jokes, were you Karl?"

It was heading towards Sunday lunchtime and soon the pub would be packed with patrons having Sunday lunch, especially in the Beer Garden.

Over near the window Paul was getting ready to ask a delicate question of Helen.

"How do you feel about people knowing?"

"I don't really care if they know, it's none of their business anyway," she replied.

Paul reached over to touch her hand, "I'm glad you feel the same way as I do. I hate secrets, and besides there's nothing wrong in what we're doing."

Their relationship had grown since that first awkward date at the theatre, and it was getting increasingly difficult to hide their feelings from prying eyes.

"Ayup!" Karl whispered to Michael, turning his back on the bar, pretending to straighten the labels on the bottles of gin that were on a shelf.

"Did you see that? He put his hand on top of hers!"

"No … really!?" Michael gasped in jest.

"You may well laugh, but I think there'll be a wedding before long. Mark my words."

Just then Doc Brendan and his wife entered the pub and went straight to Helen and Paul's table.

"Hello you two. What are you doing sitting in here? It's a lovely day outside and a tourist bus has just pulled up in the carpark. If we're going to have lunch here, may I suggest we grab a table outside before the bus load gets a hold of them." Brendan was inclined to take control of situations.

Paul signalled to Karl and Michael that they were re-locating to the Beer Garden outside.

"Well, how are you both going?" Brendan got straight to the point, "We haven't seen you in a while. How are things?"

"Oh, we're well thanks," Paul stretched his arm out to rest on the back of Helen's chair. They both smiled knowingly at each other.

"What about yourselves?" Paul quickly asked. He didn't feel like sharing the details of his and Helen's relationship, at least not in front of Helen. It was private, although everyone could see they were an item.

"We've been okay. The practice has slowed down a bit, thank goodness, now the flu season is over."

That was the cue for Brendan and Paul to 'talk shop', whilst Shirley and Helen chatted about their culinary successes and failures.

# CHAPTER 44

Lorraine kept a close watch on her mantelpiece clock. Another half an hour and it would be safe to ring her daughter in Perth. She pointed the remote to switch off the television and then got up to draw the curtains. With nothing much to do but wait, she went into the kitchen to make a cup of tea. Her thoughts drifted, she was imagining what her daughter's family would be doing right now, on the other side of the world; *having breakfast maybe or getting ready to go to church. Well maybe not church.* Their practice of the faith had slackened lately. She knew that, as she had questioned the twins in a roundabout way, when they visited last year. That's when she discovered that they rarely went to church.

Lorraine cut herself a slice of the date cake that she'd made the day before and sat at the kitchen bench. She rummaged through her mind to remind herself of all the news she wanted to share with Suzanne. Her thoughts drifted again to other things: *Mass that morning; Marge*

*Saunders' new three-piece suite; Father Morgan; the parish hall renovations; Father Morgan … Father Morgan …*

She quickly snapped herself out of her daydreaming and looked up at the kitchen clock. It was already half past eight! She finished the last mouthful of tea, which was stone cold, and went to the phone to ring Suzanne. Thankfully it was a good time to ring them, they were just finishing breakfast. It was a miserable day in the Perth suburb where Suzanne and family lived. According to Suzanne it had been raining all night and it was quite cold outside for this time of the year. It happened to be Mothers' Day in Australia and so Lorraine wished her daughter a happy Mothers' Day. Suzanne wasn't sure of their plans for the day, apart from them all going out for lunch. The twins had made their mum a lovely card and with the help of Dad, had brought Mum a cup of tea and toast in bed.

"Anyway, enough of me," Suzanne said after sharing her Mothers' Day news. "How are you going, Mum? How's the new job?"

"I'm well, and I love my job," Lorraine was quick to reply. She went on to say how easy Father Morgan was to work for, and how she was really getting an insight into the busy life of a priest.

"Is it too much for you, Mum?" Suzanne was concerned that her mother was taking on too much.

"No, of course not, besides it's only one day a week."

"Oh, I guess that's okay. Just make sure you look after yourself."

Lorraine finished her phone chat by talking briefly to the twins and Suzanne's husband, Sam, and then reluctantly hung up the phone. She did miss them so much and longed for them to live closer. Still, that was how it was. She switched all the lights off downstairs and made her way upstairs to bed.

# CHAPTER 45

"How are you going with the family tree?" Michael asked, peering over Karl's shoulder who was sitting at the dining table studying the large expanse of paper.

"Yeah … good. Do you want to see where we are?"

"Yeah, if you like. It seems strange saying 'where *we* are' when it's *your* family tree."

"Well, that's how it is Michael, and we just have to accept it. Don't fight it … it's no good getting upset over it … that's not going to help matters."

Michael slumped into the chair next to Karl, the whole situation weighing heavily on his mind.

"Look, here we are," Karl pointed out the entries to his partner.

"Mmm. You've done a fair bit of work on it, haven't you?"

"Yeah, a fair bit. It takes time getting all this together."

Karl's interest in genealogy seemed so boring to Michael. He couldn't really understand Karl's passion for it.

After two minutes of staring at the paper, trying to decipher who was married to whom and how many children they had, Michael got fed up.

"I'm going to bed," he said, "I'm tired."

Michael got up from the table and walked over to the window to draw the curtains. As he did, he noticed a figure walking outside in the dark, past Sean's the butchers. Pausing to see if he could recognise the person, he then drew the curtains. *Who was that, walking the streets at this late hour?* Thoughts of the unknown figure gradually disappeared as Michael got into bed and within a few minutes dropped off to sleep.

# CHAPTER 46

Doc Brendan was just finishing his breakfast when he heard Shirley answer the phone in the hallway. He guessed it was Paul from Shirley's verbal responses. What did Paul want at this time of the morning?

"It's Paul," Shirley held up the receiver for Brendan.

"This is early for him" he replied, taking the receiver.

"Mornin' Paul. What's up?"

"Someone's broken into the pharmacy overnight."

"What! Have you called the police?"

"Yeah. Mark Fisher's on his way."

"Are you alright?" Brendan was concerned for his mate.

"Yes, I'm fine, just shaken. Mark told me not to touch anything until he gets here. I can't tell if anything has been taken until I have a look. There's stuff everywhere."

"I'll come over," Brendan suggested.

"You don't have to Brendan."

"I'll be there in five minutes," Brendan replaced the receiver before Paul had a chance to argue the point.

"What's wrong Brendan?" Shirley asked, sensing something was up.

"The pharmacy's been broken into. Can you tell Mandy … I think she's on today … that I'll be in late and to inform the first patient. She'll know what to do."

Brendan stepped carefully trying to avoid the broken glass on the footpath. Paul was already talking to Constable Mark Fisher in the pharmacy.

"I'll get Forensic in ASAP and then you'll be clear to check on what's missing, if anything."

"Okay. Thanks Mark."

Brendan approached Paul, "Are you okay mate?"

"Yeah, I guess, just shocked. Thankfully there wasn't much in the till that they could have taken, I banked most of it yesterday. I don't know if any drugs have been taken though. I can't touch anything just yet."

"Didn't anyone see or hear anything?"

"Mark's going to talk to the neighbours. It's quite likely that no-one heard anything, seeing as there are only shops next door."

"What about your alarm?"

"I don't know. It certainly didn't go off, did it?"

It had been many years since the village had experienced a break-in. Toveringham had always been a quiet, unassuming place, with a close-knit community that looked out for one another. This incident was totally out of character. The police were onto the crime fairly quickly, checking for fingerprints, as well as interviewing neighbours and the owners of nearby businesses. Paul had confirmed that no significant drugs, as far as he could tell, had been taken.

Helen and Paul sat on the bench under the willow tree having a sandwich that Helen had prepared. It was a week since the break-in and Paul had rung Helen to ask if they could meet for lunch. He'd been feeling a bit down after everything that had happened and needed cheering up.

"Here Paul … they've got your favourite in them."

"Salami?"

Helen nodded.

"Oh, you're an angel!" he picked out a sandwich from the plastic container.

"Have they made any headway? The police?" Helen asked.

"Not really. They're still interviewing people. Michael from the pub said he saw someone walking late that night outside Sean's, but they don't know who it was. It seems whoever it was wrapped a brick in something soft to deaden the noise of breaking glass. They've found a brick with a small piece of material attached to it. It could be that they wrapped it in a shirt or something."

"Let's hope they catch whoever it was. Just remember Paul … I'm here for you if you ever need anything," she reached for Paul's hand and caressed it tenderly.

# CHAPTER 47

The doorbell of the presbytery rang repeatedly one morning just after Lorraine had arrived at work. She dropped everything and went to answer it.

"Is Father Morgan in?" Lorraine recognised the woman at the door as Jennifer Collins.

"I'll see if he's available. I've only just arrived in myself."

"Who is it, Lorraine?" Father Morgan had heard the frantic ringing of the doorbell and was just coming down from upstairs.

"Oh Jennifer," he said, noticing her standing at the front door, "Come on in."

Jennifer looked quite on edge and agitated as she followed Father Morgan into the study and closed the door behind them.

Poor woman, Lorraine thought to herself. She must be troubled by something.

"I just don't know what to do Father John. Tim was drunk again last night and apparently he's been skipping school, so they tell me."

"Do you think he'd come and have a chat with me?"

"I doubt it. I can't even get him to talk."

"Maybe I can pay you an impromptu visit when he's home," he suggested.

"How about I come around on Saturday afternoon for a cuppa and in passing have a chat with Tim?"

"That would be great, thanks Father John."

"In the meantime, Jennifer, try and get some sleep. I bet you haven't been sleeping well, have you?"

"No. Doc Brendan gave me some sleeping tablets to take only when necessary. Anyway, I must fly, a relief teacher is standing in for me this morning, so I could come and see you. They've been really understanding at the school."

Father Morgan saw Jennifer out and then said a proper 'good morning' to Lorraine.

"And how's things with you, Lorraine?"

"Very well thanks, Father John. It's a lovely day out there again, isn't it?"

"Sure is. Fancy a cuppa?"

"Yes please, I was just going to put the kettle on when Mrs Collins arrived."

# CHAPTER 48

Jennifer was on edge all of Saturday morning, praying that Tim would be around in the afternoon so that Father Morgan could have a chat with him.

"You've got the house looking very homely, Jennifer," remarked Father Morgan as he took a seat at the table in the dining room. "I remember the previous owners had let it run down a bit."

"Yes, the Taylor's. They were quite elderly, and I guess let it go a bit. I had to get the painters in to brighten it up a bit, as well as fix a few things." Jennifer poured Father Morgan's tea. "Help yourself to some coconut slice Father John."

"Thanks Jennifer. Is Tim around?"

"Yes, upstairs in his bedroom. I didn't tell him you were coming."

"That's okay, we'll just take it one step at a time."

Tim did eventually emerge from his bedroom to come downstairs for a drink.

"You remember Father Morgan don't you Tim … from Twickenham?"

"Yeah. How are you Father Morgan?" Tim reached out to shake hands with him.

"How's school Tim? It's your last year, isn't it?"

"Yeah … it's okay … can't wait to leave though."

The conversation between the two was such that eventually Tim took a seat opposite Father Morgan at the dining table. Jennifer thought it wise to disappear for a while and leave the two of them chatting whilst she went to bring the clothes in off the line.

By the time Jennifer had finished Father Morgan was wishing Tim all the best for his exams and bringing the conversation to a close. Tim excused himself, said goodbye and disappeared upstairs.

"I'll have to be off Jennifer; I've got confessions at five. It was lovely having a cuppa with you and talking to Tim. As they say – 'I'll see you in church!' Father Morgan winked at Jennifer as he said that, indicating that all went well with Tim.

A follow-up phone call to Jennifer from Father Morgan on Monday afternoon clarified the concerns she had regarding Tim's behaviour.

# CHAPTER 49

Renovations to the parish hall had well and truly gotten underway. With it, came extra business for Elam's shop as tradesmen came in to buy their lunches and snacks.

"How's it all going?" Jack asked one of the men that had come in for a sausage roll and a bottle of water.

"Yeah, all going well. Lovely village you've got 'ere. Pity about the break-in though, the other week."

"Yes, it did shake us all up a bit, I must say. We haven't had anything like that happen for many, many years."

"What haven't we had for many years?" Rachel Elam butted in on the conversation."

"Break-ins, Rachel. We haven't had any for ages."

"Yeah, that's right, we haven't. Anyway, thankfully no-one was hurt in the process," Rachel added.

Just then Pamela Yates entered the shop almost bumping into the tradesman as he was leaving.

"Ooh … I'm sorry," she apologised as she stepped aside to let him pass.

"That's alright, love," and he gave her a rather cheeky smile that she couldn't help but notice.

"Wow! Did you see him?" Pamela gushed over the handsome looking tradesman who had just left an impression on her.

"Yes, he wasn't bad looking, was he?" Rachel agreed, turning to give a sideways glance at her husband.

Just then Janet walked into the shop.

"Gee! Did you see that guy just leaving the shop?" Janet couldn't contain her excitement.

"I know, we were all just talking about him. He gave me a really lovely smile; I'll have you know."

As the girls continued their banter about the 'dishy' tradesman, Rachel couldn't help thinking how good it was to be young, carefree, and single.

"Look, the bench is taken," Janet said as they approached their usual lunchtime spot.

"Oh, never mind, the bench at the other end is free."

Janet and Pamela headed towards the other bench closer to the duck pond.

"It's Helen Shrewsbury and Paul Bloomfield."

"Where?"

"On the bench."

"Oh, so it is. They make a lovely couple, don't they?

Villagers were beginning to approve, and in fact, delight in the blossoming romance between Paul and Helen.

"Who would have thought that love could still flourish at their age," remarked Pamela.

"Well, it certainly did in your case."

"What do you mean?"

"You and James."

"Oh rubbish! There's no romance between us, we're just friends. I'm more interested in that 'dishy' tradesman."

"Yeah, he was a bit of alright, wasn't he? He's probably married. All the handsome ones are, snapped up before we could get a look in."

"Stop being so negative and eat your sandwich," ordered Pamela.

"Hey, talking about food, I found out that James is eating more of his meals now. They are cutting back on the broccoli, as he hates it, and giving him peas and carrots instead. He's much happier. Lately I've been going in around lunchtime and they give me a meal too, for free! So, we sit there in his room eating together."

"Like a lunch date?"

"Very funny, Janet."

"I'm just joking, you know I'm just making fun of you. I actually think your friendship with James is lovely."

"Watch out Janet! That duck looks like he's after your sandwich!"

# CHAPTER 50

Constable Mark Fisher knocked sharply on Jennifer's front door. He was there to make enquiries regarding the pharmacy break-in. Jennifer was a little startled to see him as she opened the door, thinking it must have been bad news (she had always associated policemen who arrived at your doorstep with bad news).

Constable Mark Fisher got straight to the point.

"As you probably know, the pharmacy was broken into last week. We've been questioning many people in the village to see if they saw or heard anything on the night of the break-in. Can you tell me where you and Tim were that evening at around ten-thirty?"

"We were in bed of course," Jennifer promptly answered. Tim stood silent at the bottom of the stairs, listening to the conversation between his mum and the Constable.

"And you Tim, where were you?" Mark turned to face Tim.

"I was in my room."

The questioning proceeded with Jennifer supplying most of the answers.

Constable Fisher left Jennifer Collins' house that evening feeling no closer to solving the crime.

# CHAPTER 51

Lorraine picked up the photo of her late husband that sat on the sideboard. She kissed it, and then stood staring at it for a moment. Today would have been their 30th wedding anniversary. There were no more tears to shed, she'd done all of that over the many years since he'd gone. Life had changed for her since she came to live in Toveringham. The memory of her late husband was still there, and she still loved him, but she had to forge a new life for herself. Her only daughter and family were miles away in Australia, and so it was left to her to not only build her own life but to leave the past behind. John was gone. He couldn't hold her in his arms anymore and tell her she was beautiful; nor bring her flowers on their anniversary and surprise her with weekends away. All that was gone … forever! She could feel the tears begin to well up inside her and stopped them in their tracks, "I'll be late for work" she said to herself, "I must go John," and she promptly put his photo back in its place. Lorraine looked forward to Tuesdays at the presbytery. Her position as secretary made her feel of some worth in the parish community, something she had longed for. Father Morgan was so easy to get on with, maybe a little too easy at times. Their weekly customary cuppa together had become something she looked forward to. They would discuss everything from the latest happenings in the village to the state of the worldwide Church.

Both Father Morgan and Lorraine were kept busy on that particular Tuesday. Father Morgan had a meeting at the Cathedral House in Ashbury; marriage preparations in the afternoon; and Lorraine was entering data from the parish contribution scheme.

It was late in the afternoon when they finally got to sit down for their cuppa and a chat.

"You've been rather quiet today, Lorraine. Is everything okay?" asked Father Morgan.

"Yes Father. I've just been rather busy. Actually, I'm glad I was busy as it took my mind off other things."

"Oh, what's that?"

"Today would have been my 30th wedding anniversary."

"Oh, I didn't realise. It must be difficult for you; days like today that should have been a celebration."

"It is rather," Lorraine had her head down focussing on her mug of tea.

"It's days like this that one feels the impact of loneliness," she mused.

"Loneliness is a dreadful thing."

"Father, how did you cope all these years with living alone? I mean, did they teach you in the seminary how to combat loneliness?"

"Huh," he chuckled. "Certainly not. All they told us was make sure you stay away from women!"

"But how can you possibly do that? Isn't it difficult in your role as a priest, dealing with men *and* women? Anyway, weren't men and women made for each other? After all, didn't God make Eve for Adam, so he wouldn't be alone?"

"Yes, He did, but you see we vow to remain celibate so we can devote our whole lives to serving God, without any distractions. You see, there's a fine line one must tread. If I keep this side of the line, then I have kept my promise to the Lord. If I cross that line, then that's where the difficulty arises."

"You speak as if you've been close to that line, Father."

Looking straight at her, he said "I *am* close."

Lorraine turned quickly from his gaze, excused herself and went to turn off her computer.

"I'm afraid I must go; it's getting rather late."

"Yes, it is. I'm sorry to have kept you for so long."

Without saying another word Lorraine hurried out of the door.

The next morning Lorraine caught the Ashbury bus. She had some bills to pay at the Post Office and a few things she needed that she couldn't buy in the village. The countryside drifted by as she stared out of the window of the bus. Mesmerized by the various shades of green with sprinkles of white sheep strewn over the landscape, she realised the beauty of this part of the country.

The more she stared, the more her thoughts drifted back to the event of the day before, the probing questions she had asked Father Morgan that had led to him admitting something that was uncomfortable for her to hear.

Why did she do that? Why did she leave in such a hurry? How could she ever face him again?

The bus trip seemed shorter than usual, probably because her mind was elsewhere. She alighted the bus and headed straight for the Post Office, where she queued for a while before being served. As she stood in the queue, her eyes wandering from the display of padded postbags and boxes to the juicy-looking strawberries printed on the blouse worn by the lady in front of her. And then she spotted him. Good grief! Of all people to see today ... Father Morgan!

He was in another queue waiting to be served by another assistant. She turned her head pretending to look the other way at the greeting cards on display. Thankfully he was served before her and made his way out of the Post Office without noticing her. *My word, that was a close shave*, Lorraine thought to herself. She couldn't bear having to face him today after what happened yesterday.

# CHAPTER 52

The warm summer weather was certainly a welcome relief after the harsh winter the village of Toveringham had experienced. Lorraine was in her front garden cutting some roses to put into a vase when Marge Saunders walked by.

"They're a lovely colour, Lorraine," Marge shouted over the garden gate.

"Oh hello, Marge. Yes, they are pretty, aren't they?"

"It's a beautiful day to be in the garden. I'm just off down to the shop to get some bread."

"Fancy a cuppa, before you do? I've been out here for a while and could do with a break. Come on, I'll put the kettle on."

Marge didn't need much persuading. She pushed open Lorraine's white picket gate to come inside.

"Phew! It's quite warm out there in the sun," Lorraine wiped the perspiration off her forehead with the sleeve of her blouse.

"I've got a brownie I made at the weekend. Would you like to try it?"

"Oooh! Yes please. I'm rather partial to brownies," Marge helped herself to one.

"Your roses are looking really good Lorraine."

"Yes, they are, I'm really pleased with them. I thought I'd bring some in to put into a vase in front of John's photo. It would have been our 30th wedding anniversary last Tuesday."

"Oh really? You must miss him a lot," suggested Marge.

"Yes, I do. I've never stopped loving him, Marge."

"Of course, I never had the pleasure of knowing what that's like, to really love someone."

It was the first time Marge had really opened up about her feelings to anyone.

"Do you regret it Marge … not getting married I mean?"

"No, not really … oh, it would have been nice, don't get me wrong, to have someone special in my life, but I'm so used to it now. Golly, at the age of seventy-two I'm a bit past it now, don't you think?"

"Oh, it's never too late Marge. Look at Helen and Paul."

"Yes, they're getting on very well … though she's a fair bit younger than me."

Marge changed the subject.

"How's your job going by the way?"

This was the first time Marge had mentioned Lorraine's job at the presbytery since her friend had been appointed parish secretary.

"It's going well, thanks. I'm sorry that you didn't get the job Marge, I didn't mean for it to be a competition between the two of us."

"Oh, that's okay. I've got over it now. Some things are just not meant to be, don't you think?"

A fleeting thought went through Lorraine's mind as she heard those words, 'some things are just not meant to be'.

"These brownies are really yummy."

"Thanks Marge. I'll put these roses in a vase later on. Let's have a cuppa first."

And the two friends sat at the kitchen table sipping tea, eating brownies and catching up on all sorts of village news – everything from Helen and Paul's blossoming romance to her insistence that Karl and Michael were going through some financial troubles at the pub.

Lorraine just listened and mentally dismissed the news that she didn't want to be privy to. That was her way of dealing with Marge. She was a good friend in many ways, but when she started gossiping inappropriately Lorraine would just switch off and not comment.

Marge would soon get the message that Lorraine wasn't interested and would move on to something else.

"I must get off to get my bread," Marge said, taking her cup and plate to the sink. "Thanks for the cuppa and chat, Lorraine … oh, and you must give me the recipe for those brownies, they were delicious."

Lorraine wasn't looking forward to attending church on Sunday. She felt like a fool after Tuesday's discussion with Father Morgan. She couldn't understand why she had been so bold in asking him such probing questions, and especially after knowing him for a relatively short time. His friendly demeanour was such that she felt comfortable in discussing even the most private of subjects with him. She enjoyed working for him and didn't want this event to cause a rift between them or jeopardise her job. *What did he mean when he spoke of being close to the line? Was there in fact some attraction there between the two of them?*

Sunday morning's Mass came and went with Lorraine returning home promptly before there was any opportunity for chatting outside the door of the church. She also managed to avoid Marge, who always seemed to hunt Lorraine out of the congregation after Mass.

Tuesday came around rather slowly. Lorraine opened the presbytery door with her key and entered the hallway slower than usual. Her bag brushed against the hall table narrowly missing knocking over the framed photo of Ashbury Cathedral.

"Is that you, Lorraine?" Father Morgan called out.

"Yes Father," came her reply.

Lorraine went straight into the office; put her bag down on her desk and switched on the computer. She turned around to hang her jacket on the back of her chair, and she saw Father Morgan standing in the doorway.

"Good morning, Lorraine."

"Morning Father."

"Could I please have a word with you before you settle into your work," he asked.

Lorraine sat down on her chair as he went over to the armchair.

"Look Lorraine, I realise that I might have shocked you last week with what I said. I didn't mean to hurt you in any way. I guess the moment just got the better of me and I had to say how I feel. We've got to know each other over the past few months, and it feels for me like I've known you for ages. I feel comfortable around you and yes, I feel there is an attraction to you, and yes, I am travelling close to the line. However, having said that, I don't want to cross that line. I want to stay true to my vocation first and foremost. God doesn't deny us love just because we're priests. We can still love … it's just what we do with that love that matters."

Lorraine sat with her hands clasped on her lap, and her eyes fixed on the tall pot plant in the room. There was silence between them. Eventually Lorraine lifted her eyes to look at Father Morgan. For the first time in months, she noticed he was showing his age. He sat forward with his hands resting on the arms of the chair. She wanted to go and place her hands on his and hold them, but she held back. His clerical collar stood out like a warning beacon. *If only he wasn't wearing the collar*, she thought, she might be tempted to go and hug him. At last, she found the courage to speak up.

"I don't know what to say, Father John."

"You don't have to say anything, if you don't want to," he replied.

"I haven't had anyone speak to me in that way for many years. I suppose I'm flattered, and at the same time confused … the words coming from you, a priest."

"Why confused? Don't you think we're capable of loving?"

"No, it's not that. It's just that I thought it was silly old me with these feelings, but now I find that you have them too."

# CHAPTER 53

Work on the parish hall was almost complete and Father Morgan had decided to open the hall to let parishioners see the almost completed renovations after Mass on Sunday. Quite a few people took the opportunity to have a look. A new kitchen had been installed with modern appliances, and plenty of cupboard space to house the Women's Institute crockery for morning teas and lunches. The toilets had been updated and the hand towels replaced with air dryers. The only work to be finished now was some painting in the main body of the hall. Helen and Paul stood amongst the parishioners admiring the work that had been done. It was common knowledge now that they were an item and as they wandered around holding hands, Paul thought what a lovely venue this would be for a particular function he had in mind.

After the hall inspection, Helen and Paul had planned to go on a picnic out in the countryside. It was a beautiful summer's day and Helen had packed enough food for a large family. Paul arrived in his Land Rover to collect Helen from home and off they went to a destination Paul knew Helen would love.

It was June, and the season for fruit picking. They passed fruit pickers on the way in the fields, their heads down and legs astride row upon row of strawberry plants. With the car window down, Helen could smell the aroma of strawberries in the air. She closed her eyes and breathed in the fresh fruity air. It reminded her of her younger days when, as a teenager, she would pick strawberries in the marshy area of the Fens. Helen felt blissfully happy driving along, with the man she now loved, beside her.

The day turned out to be perfect in every way, with a picnic in a picturesque area beside a river, and the Lincolnshire Wolds in the distance.

Fortunately for Paul it was a secluded spot.

"This is just beautiful, Paul. How did you find it?" she asked.

"Brendan and I come here all the time to fish, just over there past the bend in the river," he pointed it out to her.

"It's perfect here," Helen said looking straight into Paul's eyes.

"Yes, it is, isn't it? … Especially because you're here with me. I'd like you to be with me all the time, Helen."

Paul gently took her hand in his. He looked into her eyes and then drew her closer, kissing her passionately.

*It was now or never,* he thought to himself as he released Helen from his embrace.

"My darling, will you marry me?"

Instantly, Helen's face lit up with a radiance Paul had never seen before, and she replied in her gentle and reassuring manner, "Of course I will, Paul."

They embraced each other with such tenderness that the tension and nervousness that Paul had been experiencing throughout the day, seemed to gently melt away.

The next morning Brendan and Paul were on their way to a conference in Peterborough. Paul had arranged someone to look after the pharmacy and Brendan had a locum take care of his patients for the day. They were roughly midway into their hour and a half journey, when Paul turned to Brendan and said, "Brendan, can I ask you something?"

"Sure, what is it?"

There was a slight pause of apprehension.

"Will you be my best man?"

Brendan swiftly pulled over to the side of the road bringing the car to a grinding halt. Yanking the hand brake on, he turned to Paul.

"What did you say?"

Paul repeated, "Will you be my best man?"

"Good grief man! Have you asked Helen to marry you?"

"Yes … yesterday."

"And she said, 'yes' I take it?"

"She sure did!" and a beaming smile formed on Paul's face.

"Well blow me down!" Brendan shouted out at the top of his voice.

"Well, will you?"

"Of course, old man, of course, I'll be your best man!"

# CHAPTER 54

Father Morgan picked up the mail from the front door mat. He had heard the postman arrive and there was a letter he was expecting. He recognised the Diocesan crest on one of the envelopes and wondered why they were writing to him. It was unusual in this day and age to receive mail from the Diocesan Head Office, most of their correspondence was done by email. He went into his study and sat at his desk. Leaving the letter from Head Office to last, he opened the rest of the mail, which consisted of an electricity bill and some junk mail. The Head Office letter was typed on crisp creamy coloured paper, making it look rather official. He read the contents, then looked up and stared out of the window of his study at the large oak tree that grew in his back garden. The leaves were just beginning to change colour as Autumn approached. He looked down at the letter again and focussed on the sentence which he wished had not been there, '**transferred to the Parish of St Martha in Coningsby, effective from Monday 7th November.**'

He held his head in his hands trying to take it all in. Why? Please God, why now? Surely this can't be true. He looked again at the address on the letter. Could there be some mistake? Was it meant for someone else?

He had been at St Andrew's for fifteen years and he was happy here. He knew and loved the people; he had done his bit to keep the parish alive and he felt the people liked him. He was going to miss them but most of all he was going to miss Lorraine. Since their initial conversation some months ago, when they opened up to each other about their feelings, they had grown closer in their friendship; and yes, there was love there. It was not the romantic type of love, but it was love, all the same. There was a depth to their love for each other that one couldn't put into words. How was he going to tell Lorraine that he was being transferred?

# CHAPTER 55

Investigations into the break-in at the pharmacy had not come up with anything apart from the fact that entry had been gained by a brick being thrown through the front glass. No fingerprints had been detected, apart from Paul's, and it seemed nothing had been taken, not even from the cash register. It remained a mystery as to who the intruder was, however, as expected, Marge Saunders had her own thoughts on the matter. The incident seemed to dissolve into the background for Paul and Helen, as they now had other, more important plans to focus on, their future lives together.

Father Morgan was to marry them at St Andrew's the following Spring. However, it might now have to be the replacement priest that does the honours; whoever that might be. Michael and Karl had also been asked to organise the catering for the reception which was to be held in the newly renovated Parish Hall.

"Hey, I believe congratulations are in order, Paul," exclaimed Hans Hoffner as he bumped into Paul outside Elam's shop one morning.

"Thank you, Hans. Golly, word certainly does get around quickly, doesn't it?"

"It sure does. I'm very pleased for you both. You'll still have the pharmacy won't you, after you're married? I mean you're not moving away from the village, are you?"

"Certainly not Hans. I'll still manage the pharmacy; we'll still be living in the village."

"Oh, thank goodness for that," and Hans gave Paul a rather vigorous handshake.

# CHAPTER 56

"Would you do something for me, Pamela?"
"Sure. What's that?"

It was Pamela's weekly visit to James, and he didn't seem his usual self.

"Can you take me to the cemetery; to my wife and daughter's grave?"

Pamela was a little bemused. James hadn't ever brought up the subject of where his wife and daughter were buried.

"Yes, if you'd like me to. Where are they buried?"

"In the Borough cemetery outside of Ashbury. Can you do it on your next visit … next week?"

"Of course, James."

Pamela thought it a rather strange request; but then again, maybe not.

She didn't particularly like cemeteries and wasn't really looking forward to it.

When the following Saturday came around James was ready and waiting for Pamela in the foyer of the nursing home. He was dressed smartly with an open-neck shirt, long grey trousers and a zip up cardigan. His rollator was beside him with his tweed flat cap sitting on its padded seat. As soon as Pamela came through the door, he placed his cap on his head ready to go. Pamela filled out the book at the reception desk stating who was exiting the premises and where they were going, and they both set off.

Very few words were exchanged between them on the way. James seemed to be deep in thought. Fortunately, he knew exactly where the grave was, even though he hadn't visited the cemetery for a few years.

Pamela spotted the grave before James did because she was checking the inscriptions as they passed by each one. As they approached, she could read it clearly:

'In loving memory of Bernadette McGregor, devoted wife and mother.'

'Cheryl McGregor, cherished daughter.'

Pamela was overly cautious of James and how he would react on seeing the grave after so long. It was somewhat overgrown with weeds and the headstone had signs of wear and tear.

"I'll leave you alone for a bit James," she said. "I'll be over there on that bench ... okay?"

James nodded.

"Are you okay?" Pamela enquired after re-joining James. He looked up at her and tried to smile but she could tell that he had shed some tears. Pamela attempted to tidy up the grave by pulling out some of the weeds and wiping down the headstone with a rag she found in the car.

As they walked away from the grave James looked up at Pamela and said, 'thank you'. She put her arm around his shoulders and the two walked slowly back to the car.

It was just two weeks after the visit to the cemetery when Pamela received a call early one Saturday morning. She was still in bed, having a lie in. It was the nursing home … James had passed away during the night.

They had notified his only living relative; a cousin in South Africa, but they also thought it best to notify Pamela as she was his regular visitor.

Pamela put down the mobile phone on her bedside locker and sat on the edge of the bed trying to take it all in. There were no tears, just a feeling of complete emptiness.

"I was going to see him later today," Pamela said as she poured her friend a cup of tea. Janet had come over when Pamela rang with the sad news.

"You've got some wonderful memories of James," Janet said, trying to ease her friend's pain. "Is the cousin coming over for the funeral?"

"Yes, they are apparently. I expect it will be sometime next week."

Pamela stared out of the kitchen window, "Oh, I must get my washing in, it'll be dry by now. I've had it out all night."

"Come on, I'll help you," Janet beckoned her friend.

# CHAPTER 57

It was a Tuesday morning and Lorraine was getting ready for work. As she had woken early, she had enough time to make scrambled eggs on toast for breakfast. She stared at the eggs as she stirred them in the pan, pondering on what the day had in store for her. Inwardly, she thanked God for her wonderful job and the beautiful, close friendship she had with Father John. It was a year since she began work at the parish and she couldn't be happier. The initial fear that had consumed her when she first realised there was an attraction between the two of them, had disappeared. The fine line had never been crossed by either one of them, instead their close friendship had developed into a respectful mutual love for each other. The age difference of almost twenty years didn't seem to matter, as they felt like equals whenever they were together. Their relationship was unique and precious, belonging just to themselves. No-one in the village knew anything about it, and no-one would ever get to know. Lorraine was extremely careful not to give her friend Marge any cause for gossip, and so she never mentioned anything to her about the friendship she had with Father John.

The scrambled eggs were a nice change from cereal and toast. Soon she was ready to leave the house and face the day. Her walk to the presbytery didn't take long. On the way she compared her neighbours' colourful front gardens with her own. She thought she wasn't doing too badly with her gardening prowess.

Lorraine opened the presbytery door and shouted out 'good morning' in her usual fashion. There was no answer. She went straight into the kitchen at the back of the house where she found Father John sitting at the kitchen table with his head in his hands. A cup of half drunken cold coffee sat in front of him.

"That looks like it's cold by now. Can I make you another one?" she asked.

"That would be lovely, Lorraine."

"Anything the matter?" she enquired.

"There's something I have to talk to you about. Sit down, after you've made the coffee, Lorraine."

She sensed something major was about to be unveiled, by the look on Father John's face.

Lorraine made a coffee for both of them and tentatively sat down opposite Father John.

"I received a letter from the Diocesan Head Office in Lincoln. To cut a long story short, they want to transfer me. I have to leave Toveringham, Lorraine."

Lorraine was silent, she just stared at him.

"Please say something Lorraine."

"I don't want you to go," was all she could say.

"I don't want to go … believe me. I love it here. It's been my home for fifteen years."

"Where will you go?"

"They want to transfer me to Coningsby."

Lorraine sat silently trying to process the devastating news.

"Why? Father John … why?" There was anger in her voice.

"This is what happens from time to time, Lorraine. I'm lucky I've been here for so long, I guess."

"Can't you object and say you want to stay? Maybe make up some excuse?"

"It doesn't work like that. When the Bishop says 'jump', you jump."

"I can't bear to see you go. I'm going to miss you terribly."

She stood up and walked over to the kitchen window.

"You can come and visit me from time to time."

She turned around to face him again, in disbelief at that last comment.

"It won't be the same … it just won't be the same."

For the rest of the day Lorraine found it difficult to concentrate on any work. When it was time to leave the office, she packed up her things, said bye to Father John and made a quiet exit.

On the way home she felt the need to cry but couldn't.

It was a few weeks before the announcement of Father John's transfer was delivered to the parishioners of St Andrew's. Many were shocked. He had been a rock in the parish and was well liked by everyone. Questions were being asked, *'why did they want to transfer him after such a long time?'* and *'who was the replacement going to be?'*

# CHAPTER 58

Jennifer sat at her desk in the Year 3 classroom and sighed heavily. She had so much on her mind at this very moment. Classes had finished for the day and the children had all left to go home. She felt apprehensive at the thought of going home, not knowing what she might find. Over the past few weeks, Tim had been even quieter than usual. He was waiting for his exam results to come through, and Jennifer thought that might be the reason why he was being so withdrawn. When asked what he wanted to do as a career, he would just shrug his shoulders and not want to talk about it.

She had thought long and hard about the possibility of moving back to Twickenham but was still undecided, due to the costs involved in moving again.

She slowly packed her things away and was all ready to leave for home, when one of her colleagues poked her head around the classroom door.

"Jennifer, would you like to join us for a Friday afternoon drink at the Arms? We're leaving in five minutes."

Jennifer hesitated at first. "Why not," she then said, "See you in five."

Karl welcomed the teachers as they entered the pub. "Afternoon ladies! Finished for the week, are you?"

One of them replied, "yes, thank goodness. It's been one of those weeks."

Karl smiled back.

The five teachers placed their orders at the bar and then made themselves comfortable in the snug. Jennifer had felt welcomed at the school from the very first day she started, eighteen months ago. She really felt as if she now belonged at the school. She had never discussed her challenges regarding Tim with any of the staff, but somehow the conversation in the snug turned to family life. Someone asked her about her family.

"How's Tim going Jennifer? Didn't he sit for his final school exams this year?"

"Yes, he did. He's just waiting for the results. Doesn't know what he wants to do yet."

All the talk about families made Jennifer uncomfortable, and she soon found herself fighting back tears.

"Are you okay?" one of them asked, when they saw Jennifer fumbling around in her bag for a tissue.

The floodgates suddenly opened, and Jennifer cried like she had never done before. There was no option but to share the whole story with her colleagues. Through her tears she explained how difficult it had been for Tim to settle into village life, and how she had contemplated selling up and moving back to Twickenham.

"My word, what you've been through!" said one of them. "And we would never have guessed, you seem so happy and confident at school."

"How can we help, Jennifer?" one of them asked.

"Oh, you are so kind, but there's not much you can do. I really don't know what to do myself. He won't go to counselling, and he won't talk to me. The only thing I can think of is moving back to where he was happy."

Paul and Helen were enjoying the mid-afternoon sun, sitting under the willow tree. Paul's arm was around Helen's shoulder as they relaxed in the warmth of the late summer sunshine. The break-in had long been forgotten as they dwelt on the more positive subject of their upcoming nuptials. It had been agreed upon that Paul would move into Helen's cottage after they were married, and they would rent out the flat above the pharmacy where Paul had been living.

After some discussion concerning their honeymoon destination, Paul changed the subject slightly.

"Do you know when I first fell in love with you?" he asked, drawing Helen closer.

"When?" she asked, lifting her head from his shoulder to meet his gaze.

"That really windy day when you came into the pharmacy. When the wind had blown your skirt almost up around your waist."

Helen burst out laughing. "Well, that must have been a rather romantic sight to behold!"

"I don't know what it was," he continued, "but something clicked that day when I saw you struggling with your skirt, and I just wanted to come to your aid but couldn't."

"Oh, you're such a sentimental soul, Paul Bloomfield. And I do love you so." Helen gave him a lingering kiss on his cheek.

Across the other side of the village green, Lorraine was putting her empty milk bottle on her doorstep ready for the milkman's delivery in the morning.

The news of Father John's transfer weighed heavily on her mind, and she didn't know how she would cope after he left the village. A thought had crossed her mind that maybe this was God's way of putting an end to this possibly unhealthy relationship although, she couldn't see how it was unhealthy. Neither of them was doing anything wrong, after all there had been no physical intimacy apart from the occasional touch of the hand.

Lorraine closed her front door with more force than usual, indicative of the frustration she was feeling inside. She made the decision at that moment to try and close the door on the friendship with Father John. It was going to be difficult, but she somehow knew she had to do it.

The following weeks were exceptionally busy for Father Morgan. He made visits to his new parish and started preparing for the new parish priest's arrival, as well as packing up his personal possessions. Lorraine also was busy as she had been designated by the Parish Council to co-ordinate Father John's farewell dinner, to be held in the newly refurbished parish hall. There was barely any time for Father John and Lorraine's weekly cuppa and chat, which was probably a good thing. It meant less time together, which helped Lorraine cope with the inevitable departure of Father John which was looming.

# CHAPTER 59

It was the first day of November and Guy Fawkes night was just around the corner. Every year Betty and Steven Cosgrove were kind enough to offer the corner of their harvested wheat field to build a bonfire and let off some fireworks. One by one, villagers would contribute to the bonfire by bringing their unwanted wooden furniture and bundles of scrap firewood to add to the already mounting pile.

Pamela Yates was sorting through some things in James' garage. It had been some weeks since his funeral and, although his cousin and family had returned to their home in South Africa, they had gone through some of James' belongings before they left.

Pamela was sure she could find some old furniture that could be added to the already growing bonfire pile. She found an old dining room chair with a broken leg; a small stool, the type that would be used for milking; and a pile of chopped wood that James had kept in the corner of the garage ready for his open fire in the winter.

Pamela slammed shut her car boot and went back into her house to grab her handbag. She went through her front door which was closer to her than the back kitchen door. Pushing the door open, her eyes fell upon a white envelope which was sticking out through the letterbox opening. That's strange, she thought to herself, I didn't see that last night when I came home from work. After pulling off her heavy-duty gloves, she pulled the letter through the opening and sat down on the seat of her telephone table.

"Sudbury and Jones, Solicitors," she read on the front of the envelope.

"Mmmm. I wonder what this is?"

She had heard of the firm, they were well known solicitors in Lincoln, but she had never had any dealings with them.

"I wonder what they want," she ripped open the envelope and read the contents of the letter.

"Me? What do they want with me, for heaven's sake?"

Pamela was unsure how she drove to the Cosgroves' farm. She couldn't remember driving over the river, past the cricket ground and up Todd Lane. Her mind had been absorbed elsewhere, pondering on the contents of the letter. A couple of families from the village were at the bonfire site offloading their rubbish. She said 'hello' to them but didn't stay chatting. When she finished with the rubbish she reached for her mobile phone in the back pocket of her jeans and rang Janet.

"Hi ya! Whatcha doing Pam?" Janet answered her phone in an upbeat fashion.

"I've just brought some rubbish to the bonfire for tonight. Are you busy at the moment?"

"I'm out for a walk."

"Can I meet you under the willow when you're done."

"Sure. I'll be another ten minutes or so."

"Thanks. I'll bring us some take-away coffee."

"Make mine a decaf. I'm on a bit of a health kick at the moment."

"Okay. See you in ten."

"What do you make of this?"

Janet put her decaffeinated coffee gently down next to her on the bench, took the letter from her friend and started reading, whilst Pamela sipped on her coffee.

When she'd finished reading, she turned to Pamela and said,

"Well, it's obvious, isn't it?"

"What's obvious?"

"James has left you something."

"What!? He couldn't have. He didn't have much in the first place. Besides why would he leave anything to me, I'm not a relative."

"But you were like one to him."

Pamela took a mouthful of her hot coffee and almost burnt her tongue.

"Good grief Janet! What if it's true. What if he did leave me something. Oh, I shouldn't keep thinking about it, should I? I might get my hopes up too much."

"No. Just do what the letter says. Ring the solicitors to confirm that you'll be going in for the meeting and then put it into the back of your mind."

"Okay. I will. Thanks Janet. You're a good friend. I can always rely on you to straighten me out."

"That's what friends are for... to straighten each other out! Now stop thinking about the damn letter, drink your coffee and tell me what you've been doing this morning."

That evening as the sun slowly disappeared behind the Lincolnshire Wolds, villagers had begun to congregate around the mound of rubbish that had been piled high in the corner of Steven Cosgrove's farm. Excitement was growing as the children of the village waited for the fire to be lit. Families had brought their picnic baskets, rugs and fold-up chairs, all ready to enjoy an evening of entertainment. It didn't take long for the fire to take hold and soon a radiant glow formed on the children's faces as they stared at the huge bonfire blazing in all its glory. A variety of food was being shared around; homemade toffee apples, cheesy bonfire bread rolls and slices of Parkin (a Yorkshire delicacy). Hot chocolate was being poured out of thermos flasks and toasted marshmallows were being devoured by excited children.

As the bonfire glowed against the dark night sky, an effigy of Guy Fawkes, made from an old wooden broom and straw, was thrown onto the heap to burn, sending cheers by everyone present across the Cosgrove's field.

The night air was piercing cold, but no-one cared as the heat of the fire seemed to warm, as they say, the 'cockles of one's heart'. Paul Bloomfield put his arm around his wife-to-be; Janet and Pamela laughed together in a friendly conversation; Karl and Michael, having shut the pub for the night, helped with food distribution; and the Elam's assisted with the setting up of the fireworks. It was the one night of the year when everyone in the village braved the cold to come together. The evening culminated in a brilliant display of fireworks carefully managed by James Birchwell and Sean Blundle. Jennifer Collins sat on her picnic chair amongst the friends she'd come to know in the village. Unbeknownst to her, Tim, her son, was watching on from afar, standing at the wooden gate at the entrance to the farm.

# CHAPTER 60

Sunday 6<sup>th</sup> November. Lorraine glared at the date on her mobile phone. She wouldn't forget this date, even though with all her heart, she wanted to. She tried to put it to the back of her mind as she showered and got ready for Mass. The water from her bathroom tap was noticeably colder this morning as she attempted to clean her teeth. A glance up at the bathroom mirror reminded her of her ever-increasing age. *Just what had Father John seen in her?* The wrinkles around her eyes stood out glaringly, almost as if they'd been drawn with a pencil. Her hair was turning greyer by the minute, and heaven's above … *look at her turkey neck!* Still, they say it's what's on the inside that matters. She had indeed found much on the inside to love about Father John. All she had left now were two years of memories; two beautiful years of getting to know him. Yet again, she was saying 'goodbye' to someone significant in her life. *Was that all that her life consisted of … goodbyes?*

Her decision to attend Mass in Ashbury that morning didn't go down too well with Father John when she'd told him on Tuesday. He had wanted to see her in the pews at St Andrew's on his last Mass in the parish. But she couldn't bear it. She knew she would end up in tears. Better to cry on unfamiliar territory at Ashbury than amongst the people that knew her. Lorraine and Father John had said their goodbyes to each other on Tuesday, and this coming Tuesday she would have the difficult task of welcoming the new priest, Father Emmanuel de Souza. As the bells of St Andrew's rang out over the valley, Lorraine drove out of the village towards Ashbury to attend the morning Mass at nine-thirty at the church of St Mary Magdalene. Little did she know that Marge Saunders, who happened to be running a little late for Mass, saw her drive past.

Later that afternoon, from the window of her spare bedroom, Lorraine could see in the distance the end of the presbytery driveway. Father John's car was parked ready to leave for his new home in Coningsby. As she stood near the window holding the curtain back, she could feel her emotions get the better of her. She sat on the bottom bunk bed that was permanently made up for her grandsons when they visited; pushed aside the array of teddy bears that sat propped up against the pillow and wept bitterly.

# CHAPTER 61

Pamela tentatively pressed the third-floor button in the elevator and held onto the stainless-steel rail. She wasn't used to travelling in elevators, so she was glad of the rail for security. The elevator bumped to a halt as the number three lit up above the door. Slowly the door spread open and there in front of her on a frosted glass façade was the name SUDBURY & JONES, Solicitors.

As she looked around the ultra-modern décor of the reception area, she wondered whether James had ever set foot in the office of Sudbury & Jones, and what would he have thought of the modern surroundings.

"Miss Yates?" a voice beckoned from a half-open door out of which emerged a tall, slim man dressed in a dark suit with collar and tie. He looked a little out of place for a solicitor's office as he was so young looking. Pamela always imagined solicitors to be at least in their fifties. He was certainly not fifty!

He extended his hand, and she felt a sense of warmth and security as they shook hands. His grip was firm, yet not harsh, and definitely not like a 'wet fish' as some handshakes were.

"Hello Miss Yates. I'm Patrick Reece. Won't you take a seat. May I offer you a cup of tea?"

She imagined she would be in his office for some time judging by the offer of tea!

"No thank you, I'm fine," she replied.

"Thank you for coming in this morning. You are no doubt wondering why."

"Yes, I am a bit puzzled."

"I believe you were a good friend of Mr McGregor's, and had a great deal to do with his care in the latter years of his life."

"Well, I did go and visit him regularly in the nursing home and saw to things that he needed."

"Yes. As you're probably aware, he has only one living relative, his cousin who lives in South Africa."

"Yes, I met her at the funeral," Pamela nodded.

"His cousin has gone through Mr McGregor's will with us here in the office before returning to South Africa. She was more than happy for you to come in separately today to further discuss things, especially as you are mentioned in his will.

Pamela looked surprised.

"I'm mentioned in his will?"

"Yes. Would you like me to read out the part that relates to you?"

"Yes, please."

Pamela was tense, sitting rather upright in her chair. She consciously tried to relax a little as she waited for Mr Reece to find the reference to her in James' will. Maybe she was getting ahead of herself. There was probably nothing left to her, possibly a note of thanks, and that's all. As she stared at Mr Reece's slender fingers turning the pages of the will, her mind wandered to James and how it had only been a couple of years ago when she couldn't stand the sight of him. How he would smile at her baring those ugly teeth of his!

Pamela snapped back into the moment as Mr Reece began to read. She listened carefully trying to understand the legal terminology that was used, when suddenly she heard the amount ten thousand pounds mentioned. At that, Mr Reece looked up at her and said, "And so in other words Miss Yates, Mr McGregor has bequeathed to you the sum of ten thousand pounds sterling, to be taken from the proceeds of the sale of his house."

"What!" Pamela exclaimed. "She couldn't believe what she had heard. Ten thousand pounds!"

"There must be some mistake Mr Reece. Are you sure it's not someone's else's name?"

"You are Miss Pamela Yates of 2 Beecroft Lane, Toveringham, aren't you?"

"Yes, I am. But surely …"

Pamela slumped back into her chair. It all seemed surreal.

"Miss Yates, I went to see Mr McGregor myself, in the nursing home some months ago, after he requested a visit from me. He wanted to make a change to his will. We had a lengthy chat in which he told me all about you, and how kind you had been to him, coming to visit him every week and seeing to his every need. He said you were like a daughter to him. As his only daughter had passed away, he thought it quite fitting to leave some money to you in gratitude for all you had done. When his house is sold, a portion will go to charity, ten thousand pounds to you, and the remainder will go to his cousin."

"My goodness!" Pamela said. "What does she think to all of this? I mean me getting this money."

"She's very happy for you to receive it. She said that you deserved it after all the care you have given Mr McGregor. Obviously, she was unable to care for him living so far away, so she was very grateful for what you did for her cousin."

"I can't believe it … James … bless his heart!" Pamela shook her head in disbelief.

Pamela was in a daze as she made her way back home to pick up the sandwich she'd made earlier before going on to work. She had posted a sign up on the library door the day before advising that the library would be closed until midday. Having taken that down, she then turned on her computer and sat staring for a while through the library window, out across the village green and beyond. The willow's branches were almost void of the lush, green whispering leaves it would have in the summer. There was hardly any beauty to marvel at in the winter, apart from its spindly, bare branches. Yet, come the warmer weather it would spring to life again with the promise of its beautiful green foliage.

Pamela's daydreaming was interrupted by the sound of the library door opening. It was Marge Saunders. She was carrying her shopping bag over her shoulder; the bag was bulging with its contents of returned books.

"Morning Marge. How are you this morning?"

"I'm well, thank you, Pamela. I called earlier but saw the sign on the door."

"Yes, I'm sorry about that. Had to open up late today."

"Had some business to attend to, I expect?" Marge paused momentarily as she unloaded the books onto the counter and looked up at Pamela with a smile.

"Yes … something like that." Pamela was fully aware that Marge was keen to know what she was doing that morning, after all it was unlike her to open the library late. Everyone knew about Marge's inquisitive nature and

Pamela's news regarding James was certainly something *not* to share with Marge!

Pamela took each book to scan.

"I see you're a fan of the Village series, Marge. Is Rebecca Shaw your favourite author?"

"Yes, I love her books … all about village life. They remind me so much of our beautiful village, don't you think?"

"Well, I can't say that I've read any of her books. Maybe I'll give them a go if you recommend them."

"Oh, you should Pamela. They're delightful. Besides, you've probably got a lot more time on your hands now that you don't have James McGregor to visit anymore. Poor old soul! I did feel rather sorry for him, he was a bit of a loner when he lived in the village. Anyway, you were very kind to him, so I hear, and good on you. You must miss him, I expect."

Pamela didn't want to get into a conversation about James, so she just said, "Yes. Did you want to borrow more books, Marge?"

"Not today, thank you love. I'll come by later in the week when I've got more time to browse."

# CHAPTER 62

After a relatively mild winter the promise of an early Spring came unexpectedly when snowdrops began to poke their slender grey/green leaves through the earth on the village green. Christmas had seemed to come and go quicker than ever, with the ever-popular visit from Father Christmas, successfully staged by Paul Bloomfield again. Sean Blundle was happy for Paul to be Father Christmas again seeing as it was his last time as a single man before he tied the knot! Paul and Helen's wedding preparations were coming along well. They were due to be married at St Andrew's in April. Publicans, Karl and Michael were happy to be organising the catering for the reception, which was to be held in the parish hall.

Tim Collins had managed to secure himself a job in a hardware shop in Ashbury, much to the relief of his mother, and Pamela Yates was wondering what on earth she would do with ten thousand pounds once James' house was sold.

"You could always go on an overseas holiday," suggested Janet as they both sat under the willow tree one lunchtime. A few ducklings were paddling with their mother duck in the pond, dutifully following in succession. Pamela was finding it hard to resist feeding them some bread. However, the recently erected sign ordered not to.

"I suppose I could, but where?" answered Pamela.

"There's lots of places you could go; even as far as Australia with that money!"

"We could go on holiday together," Pamela said as she turned to face her friend.

"Well, that would be lovely, but have a good think about it, you've got all the time in the world to make up your mind."

"Yes. I haven't even got the money yet."

"You might want to keep it in the bank to earn some interest," Janet added.

"Maybe. But I think James would have liked me to spend some of it and actually enjoy it."

"You won't tell anyone about it, will you Janet? About the money I mean."

"Of course not. I wouldn't dare. It's a private matter between you and James."

"Marge Saunders tried to get it out of me the other week when I had to visit the solicitor. She came into the library and wanted to know why I closed it for half a day."

"Did you say anything?"

"Not a word."

Pamela suddenly changed the topic of conversation.

"Hey, I wonder who put the sign up not to feed the ducks."

"I don't know. Obviously, someone who cares about them. It's probably because of the new little ducklings."

# CHAPTER 63

Jennifer Collins was in Ashbury. It was a Saturday morning. Tim was at work, and she was casually browsing the shops trying to decide whether she would surprise Tim by paying him a visit in the Hardware shop. She passed by an estate agent's window and turned back to have a closer look in the window. The more she looked, the more she was drawn in. She had been thinking seriously for many months about putting the house on the market and moving back to Twickenham. She had thought that now Tim was settled in a job that things would be better at home. But they were not. Perhaps the idea of surprising him by calling in to his workplace was not such a good idea after all. It was as if Tim was living in a bubble. There was very little communication between the two of them, and she felt as if she hardly knew her son anymore. She was sure he'd be different if they sold up and moved back to where they came from. *Oh, what the heck!* She thought. *I'll get a valuation.* She confidently pushed the door of the estate agent open, thinking this might be the beginning of a better relationship with her son.

There. It was done. An appointment was made for someone to value the house next Saturday at 2.00 pm.

# CHAPTER 64

It had been four months since Father John had left the parish. Lorraine had received one letter from him during that time, to which she'd replied but there had been no communication since then. Although Father Emmanuel seemed like a nice person and relatively easy to work for, she missed her dear friend. Lorraine opened the door of Father Emmanuel's office and placed some typed letters on his desk for signing. He was out visiting parishioners. She stood at the corner of the desk which was once occupied by Father John and tried to imagine him sitting there. The desk was not as neat these days. Father John had been more meticulous than Father Emmanuel. Suddenly the office phone rang, disturbing her thoughts. She hurried to answer it in her office. It was the Bishop's secretary requesting to speak to Father Emmanuel. Lorraine took a message asking him to return the call.

It was the following day when Lorraine was busy at home in the middle of doing the laundry, when her mobile rang. She had her hands in soapy water at the sink and by the time she dried her hands and got to the phone it stopped ringing. Lorraine checked who had called. It was Father Emmanuel. *I'd better ring back,* she thought.

"Oh Lorraine. Sorry to trouble you on your day off, but I thought you should know. I had a phone call from Head Office yesterday to say that Father Morgan had a stroke at the weekend. He's in Ashbury General."

Lorraine began to tremble, and she had to quickly reach for the kitchen stool to steady herself. She sat for a moment clutching her phone in her lap. Eventually she put the phone back to her ear.

"Are you there Lorraine? Are you okay?"

"Yes, I'm fine" she lied. "How bad is he?"

"Not exactly sure. I'm going to visit him today. I'll let you know how he is."

"Yes. Please do."

Lorraine struggled to concentrate on the laundry for the rest of the morning. Her thoughts were on Father John. *Was he badly affected by the stroke? Could he still speak?* She tried to shake off those thoughts, but they kept haunting her.

The next day Father Emmanuel rang Lorraine to let her know that Father John had lost the use of his left arm, and his speech was slightly affected. He was able to sit up in bed and seemed in reasonably good spirits. Lorraine wanted to visit him, but she was afraid of how she'd react to seeing him. Besides, she hated hospitals. It had been a few months since they'd spoken, and she didn't even know if he felt the same way towards her. Had the love disappeared? She longed for it to remain the same as it was when he was at St Andrew's.

It was several weeks before Lorraine mustered up the courage to visit Father John in rehabilitation. He had begun some speech therapy and she found him able to communicate quite well, all things considered.

As she left the rehabilitation centre, she felt a wave of loneliness wash over her. Father John had seemed cool towards her. Well, what was she expecting? He had just suffered a stroke after all! A myriad of thoughts raced around in her head on the way home. It seemed as if the visit had conjured up a host of unrealistic expectations within her.

She began to wish she had never paid him a visit, and that she could leave their relationship as a mere memory.

The bus was full on the way home. Lorraine was suddenly distracted from behind by a tap on her shoulder. It was Marge Saunders.

"Oh hello, Marge. I didn't see you sitting there."

"No, you seemed miles away when you got on the bus. Been shopping, have you?"

"Er … yes," she didn't want Marge to know where she'd been. Her friend looked at her strangely, expecting to see shopping bags on the seat next to her. Lorraine knew what she was thinking, but she didn't say a word.

# CHAPTER 65

Jennifer opened her front door and bent down to pick up her 'Welcome' mat from the front step to give it a shake. It was almost two o'clock and the estate agent representative was due any minute. She dropped the mat back onto the step and glanced down the road to check for any sign of him. Nothing yet.

She went back inside to wait. She hadn't told Tim about her plans. She wasn't ready to. She'd wait to see what the valuer had to say about the value of her property.

Jennifer was pleasantly surprised at the valuation as it was more than she'd expected. She'd wait another week or so to reflect a bit more on her plans, and then put it to Tim when she felt the time was right.

It was Thursday evening and Jennifer had just got in from the Women's Institute meeting. It had gone on longer than usual as there was much discussion about the arrangements for Paul and Helen's wedding reception. The Women's Institute had decided to supply the dessert for the reception as their wedding gift to the couple. Jennifer was exhausted. She'd had a hectic day at work and now the lengthy Women's Institute meeting.

She sipped on a mug of cocoa while unwinding in front of the television. Tim was in his room as per usual. She tapped on his door in her usual fashion to say 'goodnight' before heading into her bedroom. There was no answer, but that was normal. *He's probably already asleep*, she thought.

Jennifer squinted at her alarm clock to check the time. Two thirty-five in the morning! She'd been tossing and turning for hours unable to drift into a deep sleep. After much deliberation she decided to get up and make herself a camomile tea to try and relax and get some sleep. She slipped on her light dressing gown and picked up her reading glasses from the bedside table. It was cool in the kitchen and the flagstone tiles were cold under her feet.

Jenifer flicked the switch of the kettle and stood there waiting, staring out of the kitchen window. She loved the view from the kitchen sink out towards the village green. She would often just gaze out of the window at the view when she was washing up. She would miss this view if they moved. Jennifer now looked across to the green and the weeping willow; the lone streetlamp lighting up the darkness. Something was different. She blinked a few times and rubbed her tired eyes. What was that hanging from the willow? She reached for her glasses on the kitchen bench and put them on. She looked out again. She froze.

"Timmmmmmm!" she let out a blood curdling scream.

# CHAPTER 66

The funeral peal of the single bell resounded across the Bryant Valley. Mourners gathered silently in the stone-built church of St Andrews.

Jennifer Collins sat in a front row pew with her ex-husband next to her on one side, and her two married sons with their wives, on the other. Her face was ashen.

Lorraine Thompson was there reverently placing the lectionary on the lectern and checking that the altar candles were lit. She bowed in front of the altar before returning to her place in the congregation. Although Tim Collins was not well known in the village, the church was packed, with some mourners having to resort to standing outside the doors. St Andrew's school staff were there to support Jennifer and just about every villager was in attendance.

As Tim's coffin was carried into the church, a blanket of silence descended upon the congregation. Father Emmanuel restrainedly cleared his throat and then began the ceremony of thanksgiving and remembrance for a life taken too soon.

While the funeral cortege slowly made its way from the church to Ashbury cemetery, people began to mingle and chat outside the church doors. Lorraine had just finished helping Father Emmanuel tidy up inside the church and was bolting shut the heavy, wooden main door, when she caught a glimpse of what looked like Father John. *Was it really him? Surely that wasn't him in a wheelchair?* She squeezed past the group of people slowly making their way out and managed to exit via the side door onto the gravelled pathway. She was right. It was him. Her heart skipped a beat as she stood still, staring at him in his wheelchair. He was chatting to a few parishioners with his face hardly visible to her. She longed for him to turn his head towards her. If he did, would he ignore her? She was scared to move. Then suddenly he turned his head. His eyes met hers and though they were a distance from each other, they both knew at that moment their relationship had never really changed. Helen slowly made her way towards the group he was talking to, trying not to look too eager, although she felt like running to him.

"How lovely to see you Father Morgan," she said, very nonchalantly.

"Though a very sad occasion," she added.

"Yes, it's very disturbing. I baptised the lad, you know … when I was in Twickenham."

He and Lorraine made small talk, during which time the group slowly diminished, leaving one lady, who was unknown to Lorraine, standing next to Father Morgan.

"This is Sharon, my carer," Father Morgan introduced Lorraine to her as she wheeled him towards the car that was to take him back to the nursing home.

As they approached the car he said, "Sharon, seeing as we can't stay for the wake, would you mind popping into the hall and asking the caterers if you can have a 'doggy bag' of sweets for old Father John in the wheelchair."

"Sure. You'll be okay here?"

"Of course, Lorraine will look after me, won't you Lorraine?"

Sharon briskly walked away towards the parish hall.

"You don't even like sweets!" Lorraine said, with a smile on her face.

"I know, but I wanted to get rid of her so we could be alone for a while. I've missed you, Lorraine."

"I know."

"Whatever has happened?" his face was sullen.

"I guess I thought that it was God's way of saying 'no' with you leaving the parish and then having the stroke. I thought it might be all wrong."

"Lorraine, I've missed you. I've missed our daily chats. Come and see me again ... please."

Lorraine bent down and squeezed his hand.

"Life's too short you know, Lorraine."

"I will come, I promise you, Father John."

"I still love you; you know?" he looked up at her with watery eyes.

"Likewise."

They were sharply interrupted by Sharon returning with a small box of desserts, "Well, they were very kind and gave you a box of goodies, Father John."

"Thank you, Sharon. Well, I guess we must be off," his demeanour now changed to that of a priest.

"It's been lovely catching up with you again, Lorraine."

"Yes, it has," she replied. And she watched as his carer wheeled him the rest of the way to the car.

That evening Lorraine reflected on the events of the day as she sat up in bed. It had been a very emotional day to say the least. She grabbed her rosary beads from her bedside locker and began reciting the familiar prayer, offering it up for the mother of Tim Collins. She stopped midway when her thoughts turned to her reunion with Father John and how wonderful it had been for her to hear those words 'I still love you, you know.' Lorraine kissed the cross on her set of beads and said, 'thank you Lord', as tears welled up in her eyes.

# CHAPTER 67

Jennifer closed her front door shut after the last of her work colleagues had left. They had walked her back home after the wake and stayed a while to make her a drink and generally give her some support.

"Will you be okay Jennifer … like on your own I mean?" asked one of them.

"Would you like one of us to stay the night?"

"Oh no. I wouldn't dream of asking you to do that. I'll be fine," Jennifer had said.

She went to sit in her armchair in the snug. As the hall clock ticked away in the silence of the evening, she sat in dread of what to do next. Should she tidy up the kitchen? Make herself a hot cocoa, or just go to bed. She felt as if she was chained to the chair. How could she now go on with her life?

Eventually Jennifer eased herself out of the chair and slowly climbed the stairs. She made herself enter Tim's bedroom, pushing open the door slowly, almost expecting to see him there. She hadn't entered his room at all since the night he'd died. His bed was made. The laptop was open. The bottom drawer of his chest was not closed. She sat on the rug next to his bed and tentatively picked up the blue polo shirt that had been thrown haphazardly into the bottom drawer. It was one of his favourite shirts, she knew that as he would often wear it. She caressed it and drew it close to her face hoping to sense Tim's presence. For a long time, she sat there almost in a trance. As she went to place the shirt back into the drawer, she noticed it was ripped and had some cement-like dust on it. She stared at it wondering and wondering. Tears began to flow until eventually she was sobbing, curled up on the rug clutching her son's shirt.

# CHAPTER 68

Afiner day could not have been picked as Helen Shrewsbury drew back her bedroom curtains on the morning of her wedding day. The April sun was up and there was not a cloud in the sky. Her eyes settled on her hand holding back the curtain. *Soon there would be a ring on that hand*, she thought. How her life had changed since she had got to know Paul and fallen in love with him. She had believed that she would remain a spinster for the rest of her life. How wrong she was. Helen glanced at her bedside clock. She'd better get a move on, her Matron of Honour would be here soon.

Breakfast was a rushed affair but it didn't matter because Helen was too nervous to eat. Just as she was swallowing her last mouthful of tea, there was a knock on the kitchen door. She recognised her sister's outline through the frosted glass.

"Hi ya, sis!" the two sisters embraced like they had never done before.

"Well, it's your big day. Did you ever think it would happen?"

"No … I never did. And now I'm as nervous as can be!"

"Oh, c'mon. You'll be okay. Let's start getting you ready, eh."

Over at Paul's flat things were just as nerve-racking.

"Here let me fix it," Brendan said as he took the corsage from Paul's trembling hands.

"We haven't even got to the church yet, what are you going to be like when we get there!? Try and calm down, pal. Take a few deep breaths."

Brendan managed to fix the corsage to Paul's lapel buttonhole and stood back to check on his handiwork, "There you go, what do you think?"

"Thanks Brendan. Oh! Have you got the rings?"

"Yes, I have. All is under control. Now let's get you to the church."

It was supposed to be a relatively small wedding as neither Paul nor Helen came from a large family. However, the church was filling up very quickly with anyone and everyone who knew the village pharmacist and the school's head teacher.

Rachel Elam and Sally Birchwell were at the church doors handing out the wedding booklet to each person as they filed into the church.

"Beautiful day for a wedding, isn't it?" Marge Saunders said as she accepted the booklet from Rachel.

"Sure is Marge," she replied with a welcoming smile.

Lorraine Thompson was busy inside the sacristy making sure Father Emmanuel had everything that he needed. She poked her head around the open sacristy door and noticed that Paul and Brendan had arrived. Lorraine turned to Father Emmanuel who was getting vested and told him the groom had arrived.

"Good. I'll go out to greet him."

Meanwhile Pamela Yates and good friend Janet were saying hello to the Hoffner family - Mum, Dad and their children, who had just arrived.

"Aren't you ringing the bells today, Hans?" asked Janet.

"Yes, I am, but not until the bride and groom are married … as they leave the church."

"Oh yes … of course."

Almost every pew in the church was occupied by the time Helen arrived with her sister as Matron of Honour. She looked beautiful, in a champagne coloured just-below-the-knee-length dress, made from silk with a lace overlay.

The sun shone through the stained-glass windows casting shafts of bright colours onto the stone flooring of the church porch. It was almost as if it beckoned Helen, lighting her way to Paul who was waiting for her with weak knees and clammy hands.

As the organist began to play and Helen made her way slowly down the aisle, Sally Birchwell left the basket of wedding booklets at the door and went to join her husband in one of the back pews, next to Karl and Michael. She didn't want to miss any part of the ceremony. *Latecomers will have to help themselves to a booklet,* she thought.

As she watched Helen approach the altar to join her husband-to-be, Sally turned to Michael and Karl and said, "When are you two going to get married? We could do with a few more weddings in this village."

"I must say you and Michael have done a fantastic job with the catering," shouted Lorraine over the noise coming from within the parish hall.

"Thanks Lorraine. To be honest we did have some help, the Women's Institute looked after the desserts."

"Well, it all looks wonderful. Congratulations!"

The hall was a hive of activity as guests found their allocated seats and the ladies from the Women's Institute were on hand to assist with the distribution of food. Even the Cosgrove boys and young James Blundle, wearing waiter aprons were allocated the job of delivering tea and coffee to the guests, under the direction of off-duty Constable Mark Fisher.

Paul and Helen's wedding had been a grand affair. It was certainly something the village needed to bring some joy back into village life. All too soon the celebrations were drawing to a close and the setting sun began bidding goodnight to the beautiful village of Toveringham. The newly married couple had already left for their honeymoon and a few villagers were left to clear up the mess, including Karl and Michael who stood in the hall kitchen pondering over the question that Sally Birchwell had put to them earlier.

# CHAPTER 69

Helen wiped the dust off the sideboard, being careful not to disturb the many wedding cards her and Paul had received. She couldn't bring herself to pack them away but agreed with Paul to take them down on their one-month wedding anniversary. They'd spent their honeymoon on the island of Malta and now Paul was back at work in the pharmacy. Both were gradually settling into married life, and they couldn't be happier. Helen picked up the framed photo of the two of them on their wedding day and began to reflect on the beautiful day that it was, and how happy they both were. She smiled as she placed the photo back in its place, the photo of her and Paul sitting on the bench under the weeping willow.